EARLY PRAISE FOR BELLA VISTA

"In *Bella Vista*, you can't help but fall in love with Jay, a boy with a very particular voice and a big broken heart, who's trying to find himself—or maybe trying not to lose himself—in the middle of a very dysfunctional family. A boy whose artist mother can't really see him and whose hippie-turned-get-rich-quick-schemer father only sees the worst in him. When on Jay's tenth birthday, his father whisks him off to Miami with the promise of a better life and a better father-son relationship, the adventure that finds him is nothing a reader could have expected. Written in language that slips and flows, like water rushing around rocks in a river, *Bella Vista* is a unique and beautiful coming of age story."

~ Gigi Little, author of *Who Killed One the Gun?*

"The high anxiety voice of this 80s coming-of-age story reveals the usual dramas of adolescence redefined by Jay Pershall's audacious love for his insanely broken parents. At times absurdist, at times cruel, *Bella Vista* is a compulsively readable and ultimately wise story of consequence, survival, and, after all, love."

~ Joanna Rose, author of *A Small Crowd of Strangers*

"A gripping story, crafted by the phenomenal storyteller, Adam Strong. *Bella Vista* is a gorgeous, tender, coming-of-age tale, told from the inside out, through the lens of a boy with an artist's sensibility, trapped with an angry, hollow father. From the opening pages, we're peering around the danger corners and cheering for Jay to find his way through, to claim his voice in a world that wishes him silent. A heart-thumping gem of a novel."

~ Anne Gudger, author of *The Fifth Chamber*

"Adam Strong has crafted an intimate and deeply moving story of resilience, self-discovery, and the ultimate act of survival: finding the strength and grace to forgive."

~ Kathleen Lane, author of *Pity Party* and *The Best Worst Thing*.

"In *Bella Vista*, Strong delivers a raw, unflinching coming-of-age story about love, loss, and survival. As Jay, the protagonist, flees his broken home, guided only by a weary limo driver who never stopped caring, he must confront the darkness within and decide who he's meant to become."

~ Jenny Forrester, author of *Narrow River, Wide Sky*.

BELLA VISTA

A NOVEL

ADAM STRONG

Bella Vista
Text copyright © 2026 Adam Strong
Edited by Peter Wright

All rights reserved.
Published in North America and Europe by Running Wild Press. Visit Running Wild Press at www.runningwildpublishing.com. Educators, librarians, book clubs (as well as the eternally curious), go to www.runningwildpublishing.com.

Paperback ISBN: 978-1-963869-72-9
eBook ISBN: 978-1-963869-71-2

CONTENTS

BOOK ONE 1980	10
1980	11
Deadbird Redbird	17
MOMA	25
The Summer of Sorrys	31
Escape	39
Orange Glow	45
My Fault	51
Lose Yourself	61
Miami	69
The Tapes	77
Mom and the Mirror	87
Rise and Shine	97
Goodbye	101
Exorcism	107
Start Your Engines	111
Florida	119
Refugee	121
Arrival	131
Cliff	139
Fraud	149
Subs	155
Sanctuary	163
Stowaway	169

Kiki	175	Time to Talk	261
Homecoming	183	When Swishers Aren't Enough	267
Deadbird Revisited	189	Postcards	273
Renegade	199	And Then There's an Opening	277
School	203		
Dating Dad	213	Paramours	283
Outside	225	Me and Michelle	287
BOOK TWO 1987	**230**	Michelle Made Me	293
Alone	239	Impact	299
Ill Gotten Gains	247	Why Won't You Stay?	305
Dirty Deeds	251	Fin	311
Done Dirt Cheap	253		

For
My Father,
love always.

1980

AS FOR WHY I left, why I chose Dad, if I ever did, it was more like the forces of foreign language and drugs and one guy putting his needs over the rest of the family. Money and the shit that comes from the ardent pursuit of it. Whatever combination of Mom and Dad and here and not here, at the end of the day, at least Dad put in an offer.

I used to look forward to Dad coming home.

From about 1970 to 1977, Dad would go into his office when he got home from work. The slam of the door, the poster on it was of a small spacecraft returning to its mothership. Underneath the mothership written in solid gold were the words Electric Light Orchestra.

Then there was some intergalactic sounding keyboard, and a string section. Electric Light Orchestra in sight and sound.

He'd turn up the stereo, then would come the barely-there sound of water bubbling, and the smell coming from the other side of the closed door, was that of a skunk waltzing through the halls.

Afterwards, when the door opened and Dad slid out, his eyes were all red and when he spoke his voice was one octave lower.

My Dad, the stoner.

Afternoons for us were Dad not looking for a job and me helping.

Helping meant Dad lifting me up and onto his lap. We'd watch tv together. Meanwhile, Mom was living on grants to pay our rent, while she was up in her studio painting weird line pictures. Every couple of hours, I'd get up and get Dad a beer.

In the evenings Dad cooked, and Mom would complain about how Dad still didn't have a job.

She'd say some version of "When are you going to get your shit together, Frank?"

Dad's body was this huge thing next to mine. Dad and his big muscles made me feel like he could kick anyone's ass that tried to mess with me.

Dad and I, we palled around together. That's what he called me, his pal.

And then Dad finally finished up that engineering degree. It took him three schools and two transfers to finish. He cut his hair short, he switched from weed to scotch. He started wearing ties. He grew a beard to cover his face.

He got a promotion, then a second, then another job in middle management, which paid well enough to live in Park Slope and have a kid. And a wife who can make art and take care of his son.

Dad got this idea in his head that if he could do this, could make more out of his life than he had, then anyone could do this, especially me.

Which meant everything in the house got real tidy real quick. No more garage, no more neon glow of the Electric Light Orchestra. Meant more rules. Meant amendments to existing rules to incorporate the new rules that were just made.

The bigger people thought of him at work the more uptight he became. Started to believe his own bullshit. The older I got, the more I lived under his thumb, with Dad scanning my every move, and my every move was wrong. I had a house, and I had food, and I had heat, but I had a father who squashed me under his watchful eye. There's a word for a life lived like that: "stifled," not able to breathe, every motion analyzed and dispatched with swift judgment.

To see Dad with his slacks and short hair was to deny that there ever was a time when Dad sat around drawing logos for businesses and got paid well for it, was able to stay at home all day drawing logos for businesses, pal around with me and got stoned, when he had long hair, when he didn't take himself so seriously. That's what he used to say to Mom, "Linda, you need to not take things so seriously."

Back then Linda, my Mom, called him the Dirty Hippie.

Mom was a painter and for a few years, *Dad* was the fuck up.

Those early years, me and Dad driving with the top down of his lime green Karmann Ghia when we drove over the bridge into Manhattan, the color of the sky and all those cars moving in one long river of highway. Dad's face, his big sunglasses, his long hair blowing around his face, the smile that peeked out from all that hair. "This whole world is yours, kid." He said, "It's all for you."

That memory was the kind of thing I'd forget about a few years later when he was telling me how I was too goddamn lazy to do anything right, and sometimes in the middle of one of his tirades, I had this weird moment of clarity, where I could see how what he was saying to me in the present would affect me in the future. When I was an adult, I couldn't see criticism as anything less than an attack on the blood and bone of who I was.

But there were a few years before he set up an electrical system in me that could be called upon and shocked. So by just looking at me, he could increase my blood pressure, send messages from my brain to my heart, make my palms sweat, even mess with my ability to speak. And sure, some people say they can't blame their fathers forever, but how could I not when he installed a goddamned electrical system in my nerve endings.

I was just a kid, I only saw what was in front of me.

My whole world was the songs I played in my head and the adventure stories I told myself. Because by escaping I just didn't have to deal. So this world I built up, it was from the soft comforting hues of figuring out how on my favorite TV show, the Monkees, a group of four men could play psychedelic rock and animate a cartoon at the same time, because If I could do that then I wouldn't have to live with someone analyzing my every breath. Then I wouldn't have to live under his thumb, his rules. I wouldn't have to think about how Dad changed from a fun-loving stoner to a guy who sat in his desk chair in his office with all of the lights off and talk engineering schematics into a tape recorder.

If I paid attention to sci fi stories and comic books, I wouldn't have to think about how the older I got, the more I was noticing the presence of death, how no matter how good things got, in the end, we died, and I saw it in everything from the sky on a cloudy day to the look in Mom's eyes when she was working on one of her paintings, behind all of this was the idea everything we did eventually led to the ground.

What I saw as soon as I was cognizant of it was the step by step decay of all things. I don't know if it was some sort of OCDADHD hybrid diagnosis that never came, but it allowed me 24 hour access to the detailed ways in which all things were in the process of decaying.

I never thought I'd be able to leave all that hurt behind, for Dad changing and never going back, for tricking me into hiding the tapes, for leading me down to Miami and then taking off, and the lies and the lies and the lies. And with all this, at the end of it, I couldn't believe I did it, the one thing I thought for years I'd never be able to do, what I finally did in the end, which was to forgive him.

Bella Vista

DEADBIRD REDBIRD

I WAS SEVEN IN THE middle of an October afternoon the first time I really got up close to death. Mom and I were coming back home to pick up a suit for me for some school thing. Five steps to our walk up, four colors of leaves, red, orange, brown and yellow, shadows of the upcoming winter, sounds of laughter from around the block. Right on the fourth step a bird was lying there. Lying with his face down, like he just passed out.

I'd known this exact bird. He used to come to my house every spring, a cardinal, a bright red body, black wings, little orange nose. I reached my hand out to see if he was sleeping, but when I held my hand out and patted his back, the feeling of something that was moving a few minutes ago was still. The shadow of Mom was behind me, her purse kept swinging into my back. That knock, that sway, it was a comfort to what I was looking at, that little guy, my deadbird redbird, All that made him heavy was gone.

"Don't touch that thing," she said, "it's disgusting." Mom's face, her gaze was still up on the front door, she didn't even look down.

I'd seen dead animals before, but not right in front of me and certainly not on the steps of my house. Usually this guy was so red, tuft of feathers on the top and his orange beak, whistling that little tune of his. But he had this shade to him, the color of a little bit of blood and a whole lot of water, and not just in his face, in his beak, or in the wrinkles underneath the eyes, but it was in his body too. That shade was the last bit of him shining up through his skin. His lifeless eyeballs stared off into nothing. That little guy lying there, life drained out of him like that, my deadbird redbird.

I didn't want to just leave him there on the step, I told mom I wanted to bury him.

MOM'S HAND WHEN SHE HANDED me a tissue, her long fingers, her wedding ring, the bunched-up wrinkles of her knuckle.

"If you are going to touch that thing," Mom said, "you might as well use a tissue."

THEN MOM AND THE CLACK of her heels up the walk up, no words, just the jangle of her keys, the bang crash of the front door shut.

How little weight there was in that little body, picked him up with the tissue in my hand, set him down on one of Mom's planters by the steps. The tissue and how it hung there, a little sheet that came off his face.

Nothing but my own hands to bury him with, the ground, the dirt a little hard on top, warmer underneath when I got my hands down in there, the cup of my hand, four scoops of dirt in a pile, a hole in front of me, a bed for the little guy to lie in.

Half smiles of dirt underneath my fingernails. I picked him up between my thumb and forefinger. His eyes, no reflection, no movement, just gone.

There was a gap, a space in time that was my brain telling my hand what to do and me doing it. I had my palm on that pile of dirt turned flat. Deadbird redbird's head was the last part to be buried, his face was behind the white tissue before I pushed the rest of the dirt over him.

I never napped, but that day I napped of salty sweat and the little bit of light I could see through my sheet. That little guy, that shade. I couldn't see anything else. Once I saw deadbird redbird I saw him everywhere.

I WAS AT SCHOOL, AND I had to pee. Mrs. Johnson was just on the other side of my desk with her short bob of hair, her baby-blue blouse. My hand went up, she was helping out another kid. His paper was worn thin from working on some math problems. There was an ache under my arm from having my hand up for so long.

I coughed to try to get her to turn around and see me.

"**J**AY," SHE SAID, "CAN'T YOU just wait for a second?" Her face was normally so sweet, but when she turned to look over at me, deadbird redbird came right through the skin of her face.

Started out in my chest, the shortness of breath, the tremble in my voice, I was amazed at just how quickly she could turn into something who was not alive.

"You never heard me, you never saw me," I said. "It's like you're dead."

ONCE I SPOKE THE WHOLE room got quiet, the pencils moving on math worksheets stopped, the kids taking turns at the pencil sharpener stopped, even the click of the clock had stopped.

Then I really saw the tea-water shade on Ms. Johnson's face, those beady eyes staring out towards nothing. Almost saw the white layer of tissue on her face.

I went to the Principal's office, but I did pee first.

"Principal's office," she said. "Now."

The principal's office had an orange carpet baked in with 200 years of dust and sweat, and stacks of Highlights magazines, ABCs and 123s along the walls, and the principal came in, his hair all combed to one side. His beard, his tie undone, the yellow/pink/white form in his hand. I knew he'd been reading about me calling my teacher dead. His face there, even the principal had the same tea water blood shade.

"Jay," he said. "Why do you think your teacher's dead?"

AND AS MUCH AS I wanted to tell him that I was seeing death everywhere, all I felt was an empty sick in my stomach, the dry warm of the principal's office, the burn in my throat, the crawl up right before I could do anything about it, that orange carpet we were on, and even when I stood up and ran down the hall to find a bathroom, the principal followed me. My steps and his steps and door handles of classrooms but no bathroom.

I didn't find a bathroom.

RIGHT THERE, WITH THE TWO of us in the hallway, puke came up and out of me, chunks of white and red all over the principal's penny loafers.

Principal's eyes on me, still like his whole body, not angry, not doing what Dad would've done. Could've yelled and screamed, could have sent me away. But he didn't.

The principal, I stood there and he stood there with my puke all over his shoe, opened up his arms for me to walk into. I guess he thought I needed it, and I did. His arms said I don't care what you've been through, just come on in. My feet were heavy when I stepped over to him. His arms around me, my eyes closed, the deep cigarette smell of his coat. Him holding me, and his beard, his tie all undone. His face wasn't pale anymore. He had a smile on his face. The smell of pencil shavings and burnt dust. The two of us were there in that hallway, and for a second, it was enough.

THERE WERE SO MANY TIMES growing up when death showed itself to me, but that day was the first. Something happened to me that day, just how close to it I was on those front steps, most kids would've walked on by and left Dead Bird Redbird alone, but not me. There was something about me that made me seek death out. The thing that most kids wanted to stay far away from was the thing I had to be closest to.

A need and a want to see death in everything, a heightened sense of my own mortality, I was a fragile creature in a world of boulders and rocks, tectonic plates and collapsed bridges.

But it wasn't all just death, sometimes death looked like what was about to fall apart.

THAT FALL APART WAS THERE between Mom and Dad, in their friends that eventually divorced, in the people I went to school with, in teachers, if you looked hard enough they were all barely holding on.

This seeing death in things, was something only I could see. I was the kid who was quiet when everyone else was talking. Everyone going on and on about them and their lives and what they wanted and what they weren't getting. And me, all of their talking led me to sitting around and paying attention to the little things no one else did. When Mom and Dad left me alone, when they were so wrapped up in their own lives, I was alone with myself and the world with all of its real time realities and hard edges coming at me in the pale faces of my parents' friends when they came over. It was there when all conversations stopped when I walked into a room. It was in the face of a man on the subway looking out at the big beast of Manhattan. I was looking close enough because I had nothing else to do. I didn't have some kind of special power, if they paid close enough attention, if they just shut up for a second, to the way people said the things they said, then other people could see the death I saw too.

Mom and I were out walking one day after school. Five and Dime and Ice Cream afterwards. Mom gets a coffee, stepped onto Mongoose Street, the day quiet with everyone leaving everyone else alone. Across from Prospect Park a man stands on the sidewalk talking to himself, hard to understand what he was yelling up at the sky with his fists going, like he was angry at god for putting him there, with his brain, into this world.

Mom did that thing she did in the early days before she got too gone, she walked with me a step or two in front while she shielded me from the rest of the sidewalk with her left and right arm. Before we turned down the next block he ran by us, and I saw into his mouth, at the black sockets where most people's teeth would be.

Mom said he was just crazy but I knew better, he was another one of those death demons I was seeing everywhere back then.

Bella Vista

MOMA

ONE AFTERNOON MOM PICKED me up from school. I was surprised to see her. Mom's face, you could tell, something good had just happened to her.

"I have a surprise for you," she said.

We didn't make the usual left and right turns home, we walked hand in hand to the closest subway station into Manhattan. The sun was out, it wasn't too cold, Mom squeezed my hand, and I had to squeeze back, the two of us sending our love back and forth.

She didn't tell me where we were going, and I was so happy just to be with her, I didn't care. It wasn't until we got off the subway and walked up the steps, walked the three blocks or whatever that I saw the crosswalk, the big rectangle overhang, the gauzy glow from the light inside projected outside.

When we got to the entrance, black block letters said Museum of Modern Art. "MOMA," Mom said. "The only museum for Moms."

Mom just then, the smile she gave me, usually she was so into her own work, stuck between thoughts, but all of her was with me.

We wandered around the museum, waiting for her painting to introduce itself to us. Mom didn't want to know where in the museum her painting was, she wanted to be just as surprised as I was.

Mom with my hand in hers, she was leading me through this place, and even though she wasn't saying anything, it was the way she didn't say anything that made me realize, she was making space in her life for these paintings and what they had to tell her.

Row after row of paintings that made no damn sense to me as an 8 year old. Lines that started out small and got larger, some canvases just had a dot on it and nothing else. All these lines not pointing to anything. These painted lines were just as unreadable to me as adults were back then. My first trip to a museum, the museum to show me one of her paintings, in MOMA, but all I saw was an army of paintings trying to tell me about something I knew nothing about. I could tell that the lines in-between two square splotches were supposed to bring up something in me, but I had no idea which lines to read between.

We saw the Picassos and the Monets, the Magrittes, and people that looked electrocuted with their hair frizzed all out, and the one that freaked me out the most, the Francis Bacon painting of a priest who looked like a skeleton, with his own electrical system pre-installed along his arms and legs.

And then just a few rooms away, there was Mom's painting. Her painting had squiggly lines and between them there was space that was carved out, were the shape of two U's facing each other in the shape of a stretched out oval. The things that came out of that oval, the swirls and lines and bunches of color, was Mom's way of saying her vagina was the nexus of creation. The place where all things come from. Mom's creation was art, but it was also about me being born.

"I made this painting for you," Mom said, "knowing that one day you would see it." Mom's painting had a plaque next to it that read *Fertile Crescent. Kate Pershall.*

"What can I say, your Mom's got a sense of humor," she laughed hard, at herself, knowing I was watching.

SEEING MOM'S PAINTING IN A serious place like a fancy museum where people take time out of their busy lives to lean over and figure out how things like lines and bursts of color relate to their own lives really blew my idea of what Mom did wide open. Before that visit, I figured she sold a painting every once in a while, now that I saw her work next to the work of what Mom would call the masters, there was a lightness to that, this bit of good feeling that spread from her to me. The fancy people viewing Mom's painting, the sort of conversations they had, whenever you got a few of Mom's art friends together, they talked about the ideas in the paintings as if the ideas they talked about could actually be built from these paintings. To them these paintings were blueprints for ideas, they believed that there was a place in time and space where these ideas could be built up and eventually exist in the physical world.

I tried to find my mom's legs in the middle of all those abstract lines. Mom gave my hand another squeeze and I gave one back.

"I started this painting the day I found out I was pregnant with you," she said. "My whole life changed that day. I wasn't just going to make art, I was going to make a baby too."

Mom put her hand on my shoulder, took a few fingers and rubbed them over my neck. It felt warm all up and down my body.

Me and Mom in the museum that day, the painting on the wall was me being brought into this world. And the whole moment was all about the half-awake, half-asleep tone she had to her voice, it was one of those moments I was going to remember forever.

"When we found out we were going to have you," Mom said, "Me and your Dad were still so irresponsible."

She laughed like I was someone who was much older.

"**YOUR FATHER DIDN'T WANT TO** change, but I did." Mom's eyes were full on me then, present, there, ready to take the truth head on.

"One of us had to be responsible," she said.

JUST TRYING TO PICTURE DAD like that, someone who wasn't responsible suddenly forced to be responsible, because of a kid, because of me, in one sense it was hard to see it, but in another. I saw my existence as *the* reason for him changing.

The reason for the change was a daylong seminar called Finding One's Inner Worth. I didn't know what Dad saw that day, but whatever it was it was enough to make him cut his hair, throw his bong out and start strategizing how he could take himself more seriously in service of his family.

"I've been a clown," Dad said to Mom one night. "I need to change so I'm going to."

And mom just said "Frank, honey, I don't want you to change, I just want you to make more money for us. I don't care how you do it, just don't turn into a dick, ok?"

That day in the museum I was pulled in two directions, grounded by the love my Mom had of me, reassured in just how unwavering that love was, a current I could feel stretched out in me from my hand to my chest and mind, and then this other darker presence, a force I had to make sure was addressed so I didn't get caught up in his wake.

And maybe that's when I knew about Dad, how after he cleaned up and sorted himself out, the reason he was so cranky with me. Maybe that's when he started resenting me, for having to change his life, maybe that's what woke him up, not his job, but his resentment. Maybe that's why he was so upset with me. Maybe that's why I was no longer his pal.

Bella Vista

THE SUMMER OF SORRYS

LATELY DAD HAD BEEN obsessing over every little detail, who would have thought he would have a perfectionist hiding underneath all the pot smoke no longer in his head.

I was 8. I was walking home from school and my shoulders were burning from the straps of my backpack. Tall trees and green street signs. I took the usual lefts and rights to the third house, to the big front door of our walkup. Dad, the way he showed off the locks and buzzers we had on our door, you've thought he invented the things. We had five layers of lock, some that slid, and some that dead-bolted. I was supposed to lock the front door but my favorite song, "Staying Alive", broke into my brain and took over my thoughts. The lyrics were my thoughts and the chorus was my heart and the beats were my hands and feet.

I didn't lock the door.

Bella Vista

And I didn't put my shoes away. I left them far apart, not under the shoe bench. I was inside the front door, but all I could see was my favorite record going round and round on my record player. That's where I wanted to be, upstairs in my bottom bunk, in my own world, with my Shogun Warrior, Mazinga. Mazinga is a powerful robot with a sword who can annihilate any object with his mind. The sword is for just in case. Next to my desk was my record player. Some folks called it a turntable, I called it a record player. When I lifted the cover, there was this hockey stick shaped arm with a needle and cartridge on it. I pressed the button to start the record player. I didn't know how to put the needle right on the record. The one time I tried and the needle sounded like Dad yelling and it made my bones itch.

I had these big headphones that used to be Dad's that still smelled of pot smoke. When I had them on, I couldn't hear anything but the crackle sound of the needle going round the record.

"Staying Alive," by the Bee Gees has these violins to them, and back then hearing them was like being lifted up onto the ceiling, through the roof, up to the sky to space and God almighty, even though I didn't believe in God.

So that's where I was in my head, already upstairs with only "Staying Alive" and my Mazinga for protection. Downstairs I dumped my backpack onto the bench. I didn't look back. I moved in one long motion up to the hallway steps.

I was spaced out on those steps, looking at Mom and Dad's wedding picture on the wall.

Book One 1980 | *The Summer Of Sorrys*

I was halfway up the stairs, and there was a step-step sound outside the door. That's when I realized my shoes were down there, not in the bench where they were supposed to be, they were right in front of the front door. Two striped black and white shoes.

Dad was already home from work and I was too far from the top of the stairs to run to my room and too far from the bottom step to run back and put my shoes away.

There's the shoes and there's the wooden floor, and there goes the bottom lock, the click and poke. Then he stopped. He stopped because Dad found out that the door was unlocked.

I'd left the door unlocked.

THE SCRATCH OF THE KEY pulled out of the lock, a second for his thumb to mash down on the latch by the door handle, the rattling and the door was open and the light from all that humidity outside. Dark gray cloud pants, dark coat. White shirt, red tie. The rest of his face, his big bulbous nose, his lips, and his beard that covered up the version of Dad I knew. Dad's eyes were wide open and pulled back. All systems had been alerted.

I saw it all in slow motion. I didn't move, I didn't say a thing.

HIS EYES WERE RIGHT ON me. He knew where I was as soon as he opened the door. Not even a hello or a hi, just Dad's voice in the doorway.

Dad's voice hit that deep dark note.

"You come home," Dad said. "You lock the goddamned door."

NO PAUSES FOR DAD, NO breath for oxygen, just eyes and briefcase and beard and red tie and shoes.

"How many goddamned times I told you about your goddamned shoes." When Dad got mad, everything got damned by god.

When Dad said it, there was this transformation in him, a man in a shirt and tie turned into an animal, the intersection of a bark and a shout, this one deep dark tone. I felt it run up my chest and through my body, the pull from the electrical system he built in me.

That shout, that bark, came from the deepest dark part of Dad. I couldn't believe how quickly Dad changed from one person to another, I didn't know what he was trying to do, with the guy he used to call his pal, the whole summer he was like that.

Because a few weeks later and Mom was out at some art class, painting naked men with frizzy hair. I was supposed to set the table. Supposed to bring salad dressing, put forks, knives, and a big wooden bowl out to the table. Supposed to take two wooden animal napkin holders out there. My fingers over the smooth wood of the napkin holders. Each of them had their own spirit animal. Mom's was a giraffe and Dad's was a lion. The front door was locked and my shoes were where they were supposed to be. I gave the salad bowl a big hug, the cold of smooth wood on my arms, the shine of lettuce, tomatoes, slightly crushed croutons, shaker parmesan, and just a dash of cracked pepper.

I carried my masterpiece out to the table, made sure I got the wood fork and the wood spoon. For my place setting there was no napkin holder, no giraffe, no lion. Dad said if I had a spirit animal it would be an ostrich. "Whenever you look scared you look like you should have your head in the ground," he said.

The whole table was almost set, all I needed was the salad dressing. Opened the fridge, too cold, because the salad dressing bottle was all slippery, and there was my hand on it. I pulled it out of its home in the side door, surrounded by other dressings and ketchups and mustards. The slip of the bottle and my hand didn't play so well, because right when I pulled it up and out something about the bottle in the fridge slipped out of my hand and onto the floor, the hardwood floor met with the velocity of glass, glass as in shards of glass and salad dressing crashed all over the floor.

Dad did his sigh thing, a sharp stream of air came out of his mouth. He sat back and sniffed the air, started coughing. It was amazing to me that he ever managed to smoke pot.

Goddamned kitchen, goddamned glass all over the goddamned wood floor. And wouldn't you know it. Who was unlocking the goddamned door, who was there every goddamned time I broke something or left something behind.

Every time I messed up Dad was right there. Dad had a built-in radar tuned into every one of my fuckups.

Fuckup.

That's what he called it, what he called me. What I did. That's who I was. A fuck up. I wasn't supposed to know what it meant. Fuck up. I couldn't say it. But Dad did, right there in the kitchen, his mouth opened big like it got, big and loud and all the dark places his voice could go.

"Goddamnit, kid," he said. "You're always fucking something up." Me, the "kid," not Jay, his loving son.

Fuck. Something. Up.

Sometimes it was fuck up, or "You sure fucked that one up." Fuck up was how I felt.

For me, fuck up, wasn't just what my Dad called me, for me, fuck up was a burn that spread around my stomach and went up to my throat, and some days I threw up. In the kitchen on that day I felt sick, but I couldn't throw up.

Everything else on that table was perfect, my shoes in the shoe bench and the front door was locked and the giraffe napkin holder at Mom's place and the lion napkin holder at Dad's place and no napkin holder for me. Because I was the fuckup. I fucked it up.

"I'm sorry," I said.

Apologies, as in you owe me an apology, to apologize. I had only learned what that word meant a week prior, but I said it. I'm sorry. To be sorry for something. As in a whole goddamned summer of sorry's.

Book One 1980 | The Summer Of Sorrys

Sorry, as in not Dad apologizing to me, but me to him.

𝕬FTER ALL, *HE* **WAS THE** one who left me alone, *he* was the one who changed himself, no thought about me and how I thought about all the changes he had made, and I went for it, I made the choice, I could've stood up to him, but I was only 8.

Even with all that, it's hard to look back and see myself letting all of this just happen to me. I mean I know he was tough and I know he was overbearing, but I just sat there and took it and I did nothing because I felt that I deserved all of that and more for what I'd done. When I hadn't done anything. I was criticized for every little thing I did so much that it became a voice in my head that was saying it even when Dad wasn't. That's the voice that got in my head. I couldn't defend myself, speak up for myself, because of the goddamned electrical system Dad installed in me. It would be years before I was old enough to fight back to do anything else but take it. And after that summer of sorry's, I looked for anything I could bury myself under.

Bella Vista

ESCAPE

MY HEADPHONES, MY KOSS PRO 4 Double As. When I listened to music through them, they sounded like a plush world I could get lost in.

I was home alone. Mom was gone, and Dad wasn't going to be home for hours. I walked around my house, looked for things I hadn't seen yet. Things I was not supposed to touch.

There was this photo album that had these cool red and silver lines all over it. In that book were photos from when I was a baby. My Mom and dad as a happy family. A version of Mom where she smiled and wore long dresses. Where the light was on her and she didn't hide from it. Then there was the picture of dad. Dad was in a wading pool. Dad was wearing this purple shirt, big metal circle zipper down the front. His curly afro hair reached out to the sun. Had his sunglasses on. I was just a baby and he was holding me, the beer can was in his other hand. One of those pop-the-top kinds. I was on his lap. I was so happy to have my Dad holding me.

I couldn't tell what his eyes were doing with his sunglasses on, but there was something in the way he looked down at me right then told me things weren't okay. He was lost in some thought, from what I could tell he wasn't with me in the pool. Don't know why Dad looked that way. Maybe he'd made a mistake he couldn't take back. That photo with me so happy and that bright purple shirt and Dad looking there all serious. Like, for a second the Dirty Hippy washed away and what was left was the Dad who yelled.

Another photo was of Mom, but not a Mom I ever knew. She was real young, long hair, bright green pattern on her dress. She was looking at the camera in a way I hadn't seen before. Don't know if it was Dad taking the picture, but she never looked at Dad that way when I was around. The photo and the yellow edges, so you knew it was old. Bright sunlight from the windows. Mom's gold blonde hair was not dirty at all.

Each photo was a world I didn't know existed. The purples were brighter and the faces of the grown-ups were of people smiling, but there were so many times when their smiles looked so fake, painted on and smeared, like if I rubbed on it hard enough, it would wipe away clean.

I must've moved on to something else after opening that photo album, because I'd left it right there on the kitchen table. The thing I did next was what I always did when I needed someone and there was no one around.

I went upstairs to my room, to my stereo, my headphones, the only way I had to escape. I'd put those things on, and listen to the only record I had. *Saturday Night Fever*. Had to be so careful with the record.

I pulled it out from the sleeve. My one hand on the sleeve and my other hand on the record. I couldn't just put my hand anywhere on it. My thumb was on the thin edge and my middle finger on the sticker in the center. Went over to my turntable and lined up the hole with the metal pointy part of the record player. Then came the worst part. My record player didn't have an auto start, which meant I had to lift the needle over to the record. Here's where I had to play it cool. As much as I wanted to hear the song, I had to pretend to not be in such a hurry. I took a deep breath, reached my hand out, the end of the arm with the needle and the cartridge, lifted that out of its home, the record started, the pink RKO cow going around. That little handle on the side of the cartridge, lowered it down, the two grooves on the first track.

It's gotta be track one because Staying Alive is track one. Track one was the most dangerous because it's the hardest groove to get that needle right down into before the start of the track at just the right speed.

The needle was just above the first series of grooves on the record, there was a crackle and a slight boom. Got that needle right where it needed to be and no scratches.

My headphones, two brown pods with a volume knob on the left phone and a tan strap to connect the two. Slipped those babies on, touched the cool of the silver blue circle above it with KOSS PRO 4AA in big letters, like it was written on the side of an airplane. Plugged my headphone jack right into the turntable, no speakers.

My headphones were the only way I could hear Staying Alive, hear chop chop violins in outer space.

What happened when I put that jack in, and the first few notes of the song came in. All the bad stuff, the sad picture of Dad, Mom being gone, all of it went away, and I could be a kid again.

I felt like I was in an airplane seat with stewardesses bringing me all the soda and peanuts I wanted. We were flying round the surface of the earth and where we were headed was a place full of glitter and chest hair. Planet Disco.

I was so in my head that I couldn't see what was coming. So many things to do, so many ways to fuck them up. Here's what I fucked up. I'd taken that photo album that was on the shelf that I was never, ever supposed to touch. That photo album with the cool lines on them. Left it right on the kitchen table.

Dad came home and the first thing he saw was that picture. The full story was that moment in the pool with me, how even when he was the Dirty Hippie, he still didn't feel great. He felt the opposite way a Dad is supposed to feel sitting with his son in a kiddie pool on a summer afternoon with a beer in hand. That photo and what it said to him, how even in the happiest times, Dad was miserable.

I didn't know any of this. I was in disco heaven.

I WAS UPSTAIRS ON MY BED, with my head back on my pillow. My eyes were closed. Those headphones, the things that matter most of all, the KOSS PRO 4AAs on my head.

The way those headphones felt on my ears, the connection with music I had was stronger than the connection I had with anyone.

Then the temperature changed. Opened my eyes and there was Dad. Red tie, white shirt, high end bowl haircut, Dad.

Two fingers of his on the little space between my neck and my shoulder. Two fingers pressed down and my whole body locked into him. His voice dropped down into basement territory, all in front of me and all around.

"I told you never, ever touch anything on that shelf," he said. "You can't listen, your brain is filled with this shit."

Dad took his hand and lifted my KOSS PRO 4AAs off my ears. The feeling of them off my head, I felt naked.

It happened so fast, the headphones, up in the air, and on the wall. Don't think Dad meant to break 'em, but how high he threw them – off my ear and onto the wall.

There were cracks in the two tan pods of my KOSS PRO 4AAs down on the floor in front of me. I loved them so much I couldn't believe they were made out of plastic.

"You'll listen to me now," Dad said.

THE HEADPHONES, THE ONLY ESCAPE I had from life under his thumb, were broken. The next day when Dad was at work, I went to put them in, and when I did put them on, one of the pods was hung looser than before, it felt like one of my ears was broken, hanging by a flap of tissue.

The hum I heard, that hum was blocking out the sound of chop chop violins in outer space. Dad knew I felt that way and he didn't care. Dad had broken the only route I had to escape.

There was something opening up in Dad, a hint at something darker, deeper. This thing that would come between us, Dad, and the way he was carrying on, it was like he was under the spell of, well, I wasn't sure what, but there was a pattern to it, a thing I felt in me also. I had to find out more and I was going to have to do some digging to find it.

ORANGE GLOW

THERE WAS A MISSION Dad and I were both on, this tendency to see the bad before the good, the there's-something-destructive-about-me-focusing-on-the-bad-but-I'm-going-to-do-it-anyway-because-the-bad-is-always-more-important-than-the-good, and this thing, this black death passed down from father to son. From Dad's dad to him and onto me, and how even on a perfect day, he could be miserable. Dad had it, and I didn't know it then, but I had it, too.

The picture of Dad and me in the pool. That picture, that pool, that moment. Dad in his purple shirt with the silver ring zipper, his curly hair up to the sky. Me there, the baby in his arms. Only wanted Dad to smile at me. To have me be enough.

I wanted to go back there and be that baby again in my father's arms. To see my eyes through his sunglasses, to see him as he saw me.

I wanted that picture. I wanted to own it, make it mine. I wanted to live in that picture. If I had it, maybe I could figure out what Dad had and what I have.

But I couldn't just get up any old time and take it. I had to take it at the right time, and it had to be the middle of the night. Can't get any more middle of the night than three am.

That door of mine open and the creak it made, took a lot of work not to jump back under the covers. I got out of my door, onto the landing, my socks on the slick of the wood on the stairs. I didn't put the full weight of my foot down on those steps. Fear of awakening Dad and what he would do if he found me here.

Down the steps, my view downstairs were the lights of the neighborhood through the blinds. The color I'd get when I closed my eyes during a summer day. An orange glow.

There was no turning back once I got downstairs and pulled out the cool silver and red wine striped photo album. That book smelled of Mom's cigarettes, and the sweet of Dad's cologne.

That page, the layer of clear film cover I pulled away from the book. The picture was under there without the plastic. The sticky sick of the yellow page. That picture didn't come up right away. I had to jam my pinkie fingernail under to get it in my hand.

The picture.

My legs down on the cool of our leather couch. The three am light on my two-year-old body in the picture was the only part of the picture I could see. My body was surrounded by the dark shadow of Dad.

He never looked at this picture, until I left it out for him to see. He didn't want to see it, so I took it from him.

I closed my eyes. Heard the honk of a horn from a block away. The space between the orange glow and the sounds of the street, a car door closing. The picture in my hand. The creak of the open door, the turn and jingle of four separate locks turning this way and that, the glow from the busted streetlight. One long shadow in the doorway. Mom.

Mom wasn't in her blue sweater with holes in it, or her ripped-up jeans. Mom was dressed in all black.

Mom had the door open, but she wasn't all the way in. She had her back to me, towards the car that dropped her off. When she spoke, she wasn't all the way there, her voice was half speed and halfway underwater. I didn't know it then, I couldn't know it then, but I know it now, she was fucked up.

"I'll tell Mister Business you said 'Hi,'" she said.

I WENT OVER TO THE DOOR. Mom's black tall shoes, her black stockings, her black blouse, her hair all done up and brushed, her hair when the light caught, waves of light brown mixed with orange glow.

Mom, when she turned around to close the door, she didn't expect I'd be there.

MOM AND WHAT WAS IN her eyes when she looked down on me. The harder edges of her face were turned soft.

"Hey you," she said.

SHE TOOK HER HANDS AND put them around my neck. The scratch of fabric from Mom's blouse, the smell of her armpit, the slam of the front door when she kicked it shut. The faraway smell of her perfume mixed with the cigarettes she smoked. The two of us on the couch like when I was a baby. The picture, the thing I had to have, was down on the floor. Me and Dad in the pool down there and me and Mom up here.

"I don't think he smiled once that day," she said.

I COULDN'T ASK ALL OF MY what's wrong with Mom and Dad, these two people that were never going to fit together.

"He can't enjoy himself," she said. "No matter how good things are."

A PAUSE, A REVERSAL, AND THE words she said and the way her body moved to them. "Don't worry honey," she said. "You are not like him."

Mom and the way she tracked back so quickly, to rewrite what's been written. Mom held me there, so tight, the last of the orange glow from the streetlamp coming in through the blinds. The two of us, me and Mom, fell asleep on that couch in my Mom's arms up on the couch. Me and Dad in the picture on the floor, who I was and who I was yet to be.

That picture in the photo album I took. It was different having it so I could look at it for as long as I wanted to. I could do it without fucking up even though Dad could've found it at any time. But I had it now. I lived with it. The picture has to be with me because that's who I am. It's all right there in that picture, on my bedside table next to my Mazinga. Dad holding me and not really being there. I brought it with me to the bath. The photo was propped up on the counter by the sink, so I could see it. The steam made the edges of the picture curl up.

On mornings, I had the picture in my pocket through breakfast and pleasepassthetoastandyessirnosir. In my back pocket when Mom walked me to school. At my desk. Both of my hands on the picture in the cubby hole of my desk, my thumb on the curl of the photo, the cold of the metal, and my warm hand on that picture. How one side is sticky and one side is smooth.

That picture became a road map, for how not to end up like the person you will undoubtedly become. Because as long as I had the photograph, I could return to that day anytime I wanted.

And wasn't staying in that world another way for me to escape, another activity to avoid the real world, of what was really happening to me, that Mom on this one night, was the start of a new habit, of late nights and foggy mornings, of her really not being there mentally. If she was gone before, now she was becoming borderline catatonic.

Bella Vista

MY FAULT

I'D FUCKED UP AGAIN.

Of course I was upstairs in my room, dancing to Blondie on the radio, my escape, because on some level I had to have known I'd fucked up. My room is your basic desk and chair for homework, my bulletin board, my bed, my Shogun Warrior protector guy Mazinga and no less than 134 comic books.

As for the music, I played them through the speakers.

THE 'SPEAKERS' WERE JUST A row of dots above the input button on the front. When I hit that button, then I heard the sound blended in with my real-life sounds.

Not sounds in my own head, now the sound was in the world around us, around me, in that room and through the house and down the stairs to the front door.

I was on a graffitied disco bus where everyone was Blondie and swung their gold chains to the sweet, sweet disco music.

And of course I didn't hear Dad walk into my room, but there was a hand that came into the disco bus and not just any hand, but Dad's hand, with his big pointer finger turned off the music, made the disco bus go away.

Dad was so close I could smell the sweat on him, His white dress shirt with the cuffs rolled up, his beard, his eyes back and forth looked for someone to blame. The vein on the side of his temple got so thick when he got mad, and now it was bigger and redder than ever.

I'd left the front door open, again. My favorite song was on. Dad thought I was playing some game and his face went from plain old angry to full on face neck red. Every word was a shout, every shout was for double emphasis.

"Told you too many times, can't tell you anymore," he said.

I'D SEEN DAD ANGRY ALL the time, but what came next I never could've had expected. He sat down on my bed. Which meant instead of being raging mad, he was now calm, and by calm I mean the curves and lines under his eyes, around his nose went soft.

Dad sat down there on my bed. Scary the way he slowed down, like what he wanted to say was so important he wanted to say it at half speed.

"Pull your pants down," he said.

My Fault

SOMETHING ABOUT THE SLOW WAY Dad spoke, the air in the room, I kind of spaced out, just stared out at the bits of dust caught in the sunlight from my bedroom window. Outside, kids were playing, the sound of a foot connected with a kickball, the slap sound of a chest catch.

Dad on my bed, his pants didn't have a wrinkle on them, his sleeves rolled up, the rounded edge of his arm. Dad there in the corner reached over to me. The sharp pinch of his two fingers in the spot next to my neck.

There was rumble thunder in his voice. "I said pull your goddamn pants down." I didn't wait anymore.

My hands around both sides of my shorts, the crisp hard fabric, unzipped my zipper. How long it took to pull down those shorts of mine. Just me in my underwear, my shorts down on the floor. I tried to pull my underwear all the way down, but there was something in the way Dad sat there, the way he was so patient, made me pull down my underwear just a little bit, so my butt was out but my privates were still covered. Dad's eyes on me, the way his body was so still, so calm.

"All the way down." There was Dad's voice demanding a response. His words settled into the ground after he said them.

I slid my underwear down around my ankles. My butt felt hot even though Dad hadn't laid a finger on me. I'm there with both hands on my privates, there's Dad up there and my Mazinga up on my shelf with his round belly and his big sword, but he's not doing anything to help me. No escape, just me and my privates and this thing Dad was about to do.

Dad put his hands around my waist. Dad pulled me up to his lap, then pulled my arms down, so my privates were loose on his pants, my butt up and exposed, the cold air. My legs hanging off his lap. This wasn't okay, none of it was. I wasn't supposed to have my privates out. Dad wasn't supposed to be the guy I was afraid of. This whole thing hit me right in the throat, the burn before I throw up.

I took a long underwater breath, I knew this thing was coming and I didn't know how much longer it would be before I could come up for air.

I was spread out on Dad's lap, my head was pressed down on my comforter with the hard grooves. My eyes were closed, dark and a little bit of orange bright coming in from the daylight outside.

There's what I would call a whole gust of wind heading towards my ass, which surprised me just how hard and fast he hit me. The sting was over all of my butt and knocked the breath out of my chest. The part of his hand that hit me was right where his wedding ring was.

Another slap, another hit of his hand against my ass, this time harder. And I couldn't hold it any longer, and the sound that came out of me was a baby who couldn't do anything on his own.

"Your mind is full of shit," Dad said.

His hand on me, a weight. Then another slap, weaker, like maybe he felt sorry for what he was doing.

"No wonder you can't remember anything," Dad said.

The wrong of me so naked and Dad barking these things, and all of this for a door.

Another hand. Another slap.

THE TEARS HOT DOWN MY face, my privates over the thick of his left leg. My face mashed into the hard lines of my comforter. I didn't feel anything on my butt anymore. I felt different all over.

When the last slap came, when the spanking stopped, it got real quiet. No kids playing outside, no kickball, no laughter, just the sound of the heater click on. He didn't look at me. He sat there and waited.

So strange the way we sat in that quiet.

EVEN THOUGH I WAS SCARED I still had to get up and slide off his lap. My head up off the comforter, the dizzy spin when I sat up, the burn down on my butt. Dad up there with his eyes on the part of my wall with no posters, no bands, no superheroes, just the white bumps of the wall.

Dad's hands were down at either side of his lap. Me with my underpants on the floor, the two of us sharing time. His face, the way his lips were turned down. I could look at his face forever and still I couldn't tell if he felt anything. The weight of his leg muscles under my body on his lap. Even in silence, Dad called the shots.

I slid off him, my privates against his leg. Thought he'd say something then. Or when I landed on the thick plush of my carpet.

Maybe when I got my underwear off the floor. When I put it on one leg at a time. When I put my shorts on.

But Dad didn't break. I was staring at him, sitting there, me looking at him and Dad staring at the wall. No matter how hard I looked I couldn't see him and he couldn't see me. Dad, when he finally moved, when Dad finally stood up over by my bed, I ran over to the other side, there's Dad's legs over to the door, there's his pants with no wrinkles in them.

Dad broke the silence, not with words but with a cough into his thick hand. Stopped for a second like he just might say something before he closed the door. But no, just silence.

The sound of Dad leaving, a big breath out. No sound from the other side of the door. No moment before he headed downstairs to say: "I'm sorry." Then it was just me alone with my breath, my hot wet sobs bounced off from the top bunk.

What Dad did then and the way he did it, this thing between me and Dad.

I hated him so much then. He couldn't control me with words. So he used his hands.

And I felt like a part of me got smacked out of me, the part of me that wants to be silly, to be ridiculous, this was a wakeup call from Dad.

Stop fucking around. Stop wasting my time. You don't listen to what I say.

So I'm going to beat it out of you.

Book One 1980 | My Fault

It was the way I felt about Dad. I didn't want anyone to feel that way about anyone else. To me life seemed to be much simpler than Dad made it out to be.

The old Dad, the dirty Hippie would've never hit me, not even thought about it. But Dad was on this power kick, maybe it was him being the youngest of seven, but we never met his brothers.

"Bunch of freeloaders wanting a cheap buck," he told me once.

Mom, when she showed up, it was in the middle of the night. Footsteps outside my door, the gentle schwa sound mom putting one foot in front of the other, I knew it was her. The smell on her when she came in. Disinfectant medicine smells of vodka and cigarettes. The shadow of her black cocktail dress by my bed. The sting on my butt from earlier.

Took me a few seconds to see Mom down on one knee. Her face was sea blue pale from the nightlight. Mom took her hand and pulled her red lock of hair from one side of her face to the other. The deep green of her eyes. Those eyes tried to figure out where I was in all this. "Oh, sweetie," she said.

But her eyes were not the same, there was a milkiness where before they were a clear green. Mom's face used to look warm and orange, but now it looked pale, and under her eyes she had black trenches.

She looked like she was missing something and what she was missing wasn't me. What I know now I didn't know then. Mom was high. She probably wanted to get more high.

Mom in her orange stockings, the shadow of her black cocktail dress across the room, the creak of my door. The sink was running in the bathroom next to my bedroom, so the water was coming from the side of my head, like it was right next to me.

And I thought when she came back she was gonna tell me whatever happened with me and Dad, she and I, we'd be ok.

Instead she said, "You're crying about your Dad right, You have to understand. It wasn't his fault." There's her hand with the cool of the rag on my face, still a little bit warm left from when it was hot.

I looked into her eyes to see just who was on the other end of those words. The woman in front of me was Mom with all the good scooped out of her.

"He doesn't know how to be a father," she said.

She leaned into me, the fabric from her dress on my arm felt rough and smooth. Mom's arm on my arm, there was this hum to her, her body had a motor in it. Mom's chest was there against me, in for the hug, but the squeeze in Mom's hug wasn't there. I had to close my eyes when she went in for the kiss, and couldn't stand to see that pale face of hers.

"G'night, gorgeous," she said.

Book One 1980 | My Fault

Her lips on my cheek pulled away, the shadow of dress and her heels over to my door, my door shut. Me there in bed in the middle of the cool blue light from the nightlight. All I had was the tall round shadow of Mazinga not able to protect me from what came next.

Dad, that day, when he hit me just kept telling me how full of shit I was, how stupid, and that combined with the spanking, it killed the young in me, killed the part of me that wanted to goof off, even though there was work to be done, Dad was trying to make me into him, and he'd done it, he killed off the part of me that was a kid, and what was left was someone who ran after death and darkness. There was a quiet death in me that day, a death I am still coming back from.

Me there, that was the first time for a bunch of things, I know it was the first time that my fear of him went to another place, it went to the idea of him forcing me to do something I didn't want to do. And that was a thing with him, if I didn't want to do it, if he couldn't sweet talk me into it, then he would force his body to do what he wanted me to do. And after that, lying in bed and looking up at the wood grain of my top bunk. I knew I was going to be the kid that sat there and let life take over him and not the other way around.

First him, then her. This going to bed and feel like I was the only one who cared about me, who knew how it felt. One parent in the clouds and the other hell bent on ambition, order and rage.

Almost nine years old and already I was beginning to feel like I would have to raise myself.

Bella Vista

LOSE YOURSELF

MOM CALLED ME UP to her studio, from upstairs. I was in my underwear.

She never did this, never called out for me. Unless I was in trouble.

Mom's studio on a Tuesday morning, something magical.

Mom moved differently up here. I don't know if it was the light or she was doing what she was born to do, but she was way more patient. Mom's desk lamp had this green bend in the arm, and the lamp made a white glow on the canvas next to her. She put her hand on the seat of the stool. She was wearing her wedding ring. Which meant, for now, Mom and Dad were all good.

When she spoke, it was at half-awake dream speed. "Hop on up," she said. "I want to paint you."

All the things in the world, and she wanted to paint me.

Nothing better than being across from her. Up in her studio. In my underwear. On the ripped-up stool, duct tape on the seat scratchy on my butt.

Mom, one long strand of red hair down the middle of her face. Her skin, white milk mixed with a shade of red.

Mom right there, in that light doing what she loved to do most, she had some kind of special holy light coming out of her then. I saw the way she saw the world that afternoon. The sun in the view out the window, a few trees, a dozen leaves and a big cloud.

Steam came up from Mom's mug of coffee on her desk. By the print of the woman lying down in a wheat field leaning towards a house that looks like it holds all the wealth in the world. So slow the way she sat up, took two hands to pull back her straggly strands of hair, then a quick burst of finger twists to jam her hair into a rubber band. When she leaned forward, you could see the hunch in her back, it was part of her trance, the curl of her finger around a brush. The slow way her hand passed from the pot of black paint to her canvas. Long tip wet with black paint. A trance from paint to canvas, from brush to water, black to white.

A warmth in my chest spread out to the rest of my body. Cold outside but warm up in Mom's studio.

So warm I could've sat there forever.

Mom's black glasses were down on the tip of her nose. Mom's eyes weren't just blue and weren't just green, they were hazel. Mom sat up there, calm not just in her eyes but in her whole body too.

When I sat back on the stool, there was the reflection of her hand in her mason jar.

Mom's reflection puffed up with water.

In that moment I saw how mom saw the world. Mom's hand in the reflection was slow and long, scratching out something, like if she drew enough new lines, it could write over what was wrong.

The back and forth of her eyes, the way she loved the world. Her eyes were how she loved me.

I KNEW SHE WAS PAINTING ME, but I didn't know what I looked like on her canvas. Mom and the curlicues in her hand movements. Figured that was for my curly hair, and her scratched out hand movements were for my eyebrows.

I was squirming, the kid motor inside me didn't want to sit still. Mom's voice with a little bit of mad under it.

"It helps if you pick a spot," she said.

When Mom said that, I knew that part of her, or I was reminded of that, she painted all the time, this is what she did. All this time Mom had all kinds of patience, but just up here, once we got downstairs away from the easels and brushes and paint, her patience went away too.

But I was nine years old, no way I could've sat still for that long.

The glasses at the end of her nose had the reflection of the white square of her canvas.

Her voice in the middle of the room quiet, "Stare at the spot until all you are is breath," she said, "Lose yourself."

I was in the corner of the room sitting on a stool. So hard for me to sit still.

Why would I lose myself when I had Mom right there in front of her easel, the bench of paint buckets, jars and brushes. In the corner by the window, with the light hitting her, the window with a whole lot of dirt and grime. The shapes of the two out-of-focus green and yellow leaves moved, like breath.

Mom right there, taking her time in the long movements she made with her brush. Every inch of me being seen by the only person who could really see me.

And even though this is utterly impossible, for a second, in my blissed out child mind, it was a quiet like for a second everyone in New York City everyone shut up. The bend of her back over the canvas. Her teal shirt with a little bit of ash from the cigarette that she didn't smoke. She let it sit in the ashtray until the long paper burned off in a long tube.

Those leaves, Mom's eyes, all the attention, the whole room not going anywhere in a hurry. I did what Mom said, I got to a spot where I was a body with breath going in and out. Two hours, normally such a long time, but being drawn by Mom like I was, I could've sat there all day.

Mom and a brush and all the time in the world to make me into something new.

Don't know where I went. Off on one of those leaves, I guess. But there was something about Mom and it pulled me back. The sweetness in her voice was drawn out in one long breath.

"Sometimes," Mom said. "I love you so much it kills me."

YELLOW AND GREEN SPLASHES OF color, and the wind outside. I could fool myself into thinking those leaves were moving from my breath, but they weren't. Me there, my body on the stool, the long line of my throat down to my stomach. A squeeze, an ache.

I could've focused on how much she loved me, but Mom couldn't just leave it at that. She had to say I was killing her.

Mom, couldn't just let a moment be a moment, she always had to tell me the truth.

"Mom," I said, and there was a break in my voice. "What do you see when you paint me?"

Mom got out of her lean forward. She slid her glasses back up over her eyes. The Green Moon irises of hers weren't big anymore. Her eyes were shut tight, trying to think of the right words to say. The lines of worry were back on her face. There was no steam coming from her coffee, no more color in the green and yellow leaves outside.

Mom's cigarette between her thumb and forefinger, her nails were all chewed up. Her eyes weren't on me, they were down on her canvas.

"I see a boy who breaks," she said.

Mom, when she said those words, my heart, the place I feel things, was down in my stomach. Mom had to have someone else living inside of her.

That's the only way I could make sense of it back then. To me, then, that was the only way she could say I was someone who broke. It had to be. Someone had moved into her brain but hadn't fully taken over yet.

I was so wrapped up in her painting me I didn't notice any of this in her until she said those words. After she said it, I broke, I saw Mom's dark side all over her face.

Someone else in Mom's back hunched over her canvas. Someone else in the slits of her eyes shut tight. In my head I was going on about how good it felt to have someone paying attention to me. Mom and where I was in all of this. Mom was the only one who cared about me, and sooner or later I was going to lose her.

A few weeks later, I was home, fake sick from school. The woman who used to be my Mom was asleep. Don't know what time she came back the night before. Dad was at work. Me and an empty house. Which meant I had to sneak upstairs to see what Mom was working on.

There I was, me and my hand on the cold of the door to Mom's studio.

Pushed open the big door and there were her paint cans, her swollen journals, her ashtrays full of butts.

The first part of the studio was the way it was when Mom painted me. The afternoon Mom taught me how to sit still.

But the other half of her studio had this thing. Three boards with hinges, stood up. Three wood panels. Plywood and brass. Over on the other side of the studio, turned away from me so I could only see the back.

Mom's painting. A triptych. She'd told me about it a few days before breakfast. When she said that the word, all kinds of weird things happened with her tongue and her teeth. Mom with her coffee and her cigarette, her eyes red as they'd been every morning lately.

The triptych, the three wood panels stood up on the back half of Mom's studio. stood up in a zig zag, three panels.

I didn't see any of me in there, no proof that she ever painted me. At first I didn't know what I was looking at, a brown base paint color, white lines, knuckles bones and teeth, over and over. This triptych was a mystery I could pull around myself, like some kind of sleeping bag.

I HAD TO GET WAY BACK in the corner to see it, but it was there. I had to stand up on the table pushed in the corner and there it was, under the window I looked out at, the one with the two leaves being moved by the air vent just below them. That air made it look like they were breathing.

What I saw, a shadow, the curve line, a little thing I recognized, a line became the outline of my face, then the curlicued lines of my hair. The day she painted me. The long line of my face etched onto all three panels of the Triptych, the little nick in my ear from when

I cut it when I was a baby, right there on the canvas, the tufts of my curly hair stretched out across three panels.

And it was only then I saw what she was trying to do.

Me and the knuckles and the teeth and bones, the shadow of me. The feeling got to me again, all that warm spread out in my chest. So much I could have stayed there forever.

The triptych was the whole world, her world, and I was right there the whole time, right in the middle of Mom's universe.

Her painting me, the triptych, that was the last time we were like that, she moved one way and I moved another and it had everything to do with Dad's vision of Miami.

MIAMI

DAD'S CAR LOOKED LIKE a bone white whale lying on his side. There were tools to kill this whale, poles with sharp tips, and all of these things were covered in a dark red. All that red inside a white whale. That color of red was all over the inside of Dad's white Chrysler Cordoba. The seats and the carpet were the color of whale blood. I was nine.

Dad had to go through this whole ritual before he started his car. Check the headlights, check the levels of oil and antifreeze, even record the mileage in his notebook. Once he did that, he got his hand, the knuckle and thumb, and pressed down on the big Chrysler key, turned it into the slot below the steering wheel. The quick roar of the engine starting up. His hand next to me pulled the lever from P to D. Violin music met up with the cold of New York City. Took a few minutes for the heat vents to blow out warm air.

Dad's can't-hold-it-back half-smile. The two of us, the Chrysler Cordoba. We didn't just drive, we glided into the city. We took the Gowanus Expressway to the Upper West Side.

Manhattan and buildings so high I couldn't see the tops.

He turned into this brown brick parking garage, slid a card into the slot of a big yellow box with a light on top and this board with orange stripes lifted up and let us in. We drove down a few floors and Dad had to turn on the light, it got so dark. We followed the curl of the ramp down to a parking spot on the bottom floor.

With the engine off, we both unbuckled. I got my body over to the side, by the door.

RIGHT THERE, IN THE BOTTOM of the parking lot. I didn't see this moment for what it was. The two of us about to start the thing that would change us.

The look on Dad's face he must have learned from sales school, the whole I-won't-get-excited-unless-you-get-excited deal.

"I've got something for you," he said.

Out my window the dark quiet of the bottom floor. He didn't start the car, didn't put the key in the ignition. He was right there in front of me, with a stupid smile on his face. He did the thing that he did when he was about to tell me something important. He put his hand on my shoulder, held it there like what he was going to say next mattered.

"Miami," Dad said.

There was something in Dad's face, a telling after months of waiting. Like he'd stood in front of his mirror every morning for months and practiced.

"We're moving to Miami," he said.

And if before he couldn't hold back the happiness, now he had light coming out of him, making his words melt. Dad got his hand around my back, he was making small circles.

"Think about it," he said. "Beautiful beaches, warm sun." Dad was doing what he had to do, paint the perfect picture and get me to fall for it.

"You should see this house," he said. "It's got a swimming pool *and* a tennis court." Dad held his hand around an imaginary tennis racket.

"Here's the best part," Dad said. "The house is on Bella Vista Avenue. Bella Vista means 'Beautiful View.'"

Even in all his joy, there was an empty in Dad the absence of a person, Mom. "What about Mom?" I said.

It felt good to say that.

The look on Dad's face was a salesman wanting to close the deal. Talking one thing, meaning another. "Oh, you can't tell Mom about Miami," he said. "It's a surprise."

Then I knew, in the middle of Dad's plan, I was making a choice. I was picking Dad over Mom.

DAD, HE BACKED UP A bit. He'd heard what he said about Mom, how she wasn't even in this plan. He couldn't look at me when he said it, he turned to the window.

"Mom can still paint in Miami," he said.

I saw it, felt it even, the distance we were putting me and him away from Mom, how one story can open up a hole in the three of us, and now it was open, none of us could put it back together.

I couldn't see her painting her triptychs in Miami. "Let me tell you how it all got started," he said.

Dad told me about how he'd try to get a deal on an industrial-sized unit bound for San Salvador and how it would end up in San Diego, and unless you had permission from the Panamanians, nothing would happen. You'd pay your money, but if no one had the permits you couldn't get it shipped, and if they did have the permits, no one could speak the language.

"The right guy could really clean up," Dad said. "And I'm that guy."

Dad, he didn't want to tell me this in the office with the whole company listening, he waited until we were twelve stories underground at the bottom of a parking garage. Dad and his promise of taking me into his work, we never even made it inside.

"We're gonna be rich," he said. His face, it was the first time I'd ever seen him like that. He wasn't forty-whatever, he was the same age as me.

But there was a hole in the middle of his plan, and it wasn't just Mom being out of the picture.

"I'm going to learn Spanish," he said. "And that's where you come in."

The catch, the thing that made all the difference, this wasn't just on Dad, it involved me too. And did I tell him that I wanted to stay here, did I tell him I didn't want to leave Mom? No.

Here's the thing about Miami where Dad had me, there was a hope that this thing between me and Dad could be fixed, that I could become the son he always wanted.

So here's my part, the part where I can very easily says where I added to this fucked up mixture, this balance of chemicals in personalities, it was only a matter of time, a Mom too far away, a Dad with his own ambitions, and somewhere in the middle was me, and now I had to make a choice, and I chose Dad over Mom. I could've talked to her, but I didn't.

"I'll do anything," is what I said. I could've held out for more, I could've made him wait, but I didn't. Dad sold Miami to me, and I bought the whole rotten package.

Dad right there, had this team mentality to him. And in spite of everything he wanted me more than Mom did.

Dad laid out his whole plan.

"To learn Spanish, I need these foreign language tapes," Dad said. "It's a thing now, you can learn a language in your car."

"There's twelve of them. One per week. Twelve tapes in twelve weeks."

"Mom can't see the tapes," he said. "I need you to hide them from her so in twelve weeks I can learn enough Spanish to get us down there and start making a killing."

Then he does this thing, never in a million years would I thought he would've done a thing like this. Dad took his arms and wrapped them around my chest. Dad lifts me up under my arms, over the gearshift, onto his lap.

Dad's there, with his arms around me kissing my ear, like we've never been anything but loving father and son.

"Who's my guy," he said. "Who's my pal?"

And I close my eyes, down here in the middle of all this dark. There's the smell of oil and tires, but also the smell of Dad, some kind of sweet leather smell, and it's dark and the future is scary. But Dad is here and he's the Dad I want and I'm the son he wants. I don't want to go home, I don't want to hide tapes, and I don't care if he means it or not, I want to stay here, just the two of us, Dad with his arms around me, forever his guy, forever his pal.

So you're thinking, how did you choose your Dad over your Mom, did you make your decision based on which parent gave you the best sales pitch? And yeah, that sounds like a good way to do it, but you see the difference was, with Mom there wasn't even a sales pitch.

She didn't even know it was happening. And even though I didn't realize it, couldn't realize just how important my non-decision that was a decision type of decision was, the fact that Mom didn't even offer up a sales pitch, the person in control of that was out late every night, chasing down fame and the secret of who she was.

Bella Vista

THE TAPES

FOR DAD'S PLAN TO happen, for Miami to happen, I had to deal with the tapes, all twelve of them. I had to hide them. Every day after school I went straight home and looked in the mailbox at the top of our stairs, hoping to god that Mom hadn't beaten me to it.

The first tape arrived in a manila envelope the color of a warm Miami sun, like the tape was made by people who sat in the sun and drank coconut milk all day.

I was down on the sidewalk. Walked up the steps, got up on my tiptoes to the mailbox, put my hand on the hard edges of the manila envelope.

Went inside, locked the door behind me, shut out the bird sounds from outside. The inside was Mama-Needs-Quiet. I went up to my room, walked by the picture of Dad and his Karmann

Ghia. Upstairs on my windowsill Mazinga squinted behind his sword and shield I locked the door. I wasn't taking any chances.

Got my finger around the clasp of the thing that kept the envelope closed, bent the metal back, pulled the flap open, a shadow of a tape and a book. Got my hand on the front of the book and slid it out.

Berlitz international language series it said on the cover. Bright yellow and burnt orange of the Spanish flag on a navy-blue sea. Bright sun hanging in a triangle over a boat, LEARN SPANISH, the tape said. Tape 1, Vocabulary.

I got the clear plastic wrap off the cassette tape, pulled the tape out of the case, put it into my stereo. Slid on my duct tape fixed headphones. The hum of the stereo was all around my head. I hit play.

"Repeten por favor," a very polite Spanish man voice said. "Sandwich de jamon. Ham sandwich."

I could see me and Mom and Dad outside a cafe on some bright Miami street. Me ordering a ham sandwich in perfect Spanish. The waiter took my order like I was a cultured man of the world.

I hit stop on my tape player, hit the eject button, took the tape out. Put it back in the case and into the envelope. I hid it behind my back when I walked by Mom's room.

Mom had been sleeping all day, she could get up at any second and find me, and ruin the surprise.

The place I was supposed to hide the tape was under Dad's bar.

Book One 1980 | The Tapes

Dad's bar, Dad's Monday through Friday deal: Two ice cubes on silver tongs, into two fingers of bourbon. The first time he said "fingers," I thought he poured bourbon right over his two fingers in the glass.

The cabinet was one of dad's first splurges, leather panels and ceramic handles. underneath Dad's bar had two knobs the same silver as the tongs. Everything of Dad's just had to match. I got my fingers around the knob, pulled it open, and the air back there smelled like the sweet sick smell of booze, which gave me the little bit of warm before the throw up feeling.

There were all kinds of bottles in Dad's cabinet: a fancy one with red wax, an old French pink and purple one, and if I wasn't on my mission, I'd twist off the cap just to see if a genie came out.

I put the envelope all the way in the back, and it made all matter of tinny bottle clank sounds ensued, small bottles, large bottles, more than a few mini bottles, a lot of sound, but after a second the bottles settled and none fell over. I pushed that envelope all the way in the back of the cabinet until I couldn't see it. I closed the cabinet door. I took a quick look upstairs to see if Mom was up.

There are quiets you can fall asleep to and there are quiets where something can come roaring out of, and this was one of those times, because out of that quiet came the loud trumpet sound of Mom blowing her nose. I got out of there fast.

THE WHOLE REST OF THE day I kept checking the cabinet to see if the tape was still there. I must've done ok, because when I woke up and checked on the envelope the next morning it was gone.

The next few weeks, I hid the Vocabulary Builder tape, the Past and Present tape, hid the Subjunctive tape just fine. It was getting easier, this hiding. I mean I still got the sick feeling in my stomach when I opened the cabinet, but I felt like for the first time I wasn't a fuck up.

Things were going well until the day I turned the corner home from school and saw the orange of Mom's bathrobe on the front porch.

Two months prior, she'd never go outside in anything less than high heels and a black dress, but during this phase of Mom, she walked around like this all day.

Mom up at the top of the stairs, when I walked home. On the front step with a cigarette going. First time I'd seen her in days. Mom's orange robe made her skin look more pink than normal. Her eyes nose and chin were all tensed up into one angry muscle. Red hair splashed around her shoulders. I went in for a hug. She had her hands behind her back and she pulled this thing out.

This thing, for a second I actually thought she had bought me a present, the same navy blue as the tapes I'd been hiding, and when I saw that color, I got the sick feeling in my stomach again.

A carrying case. A little plastic briefcase, to put all sixteen tapes in, enough Spanish for the three of us to drive down to Miami and live in a house with a swimming pool.

"Looking for this?" Mom said. There was a crease in her forehead and the little bit of lost in her face she got when she painted for so long she didn't know who she was.

All those weeks of hiding and now I was caught. I couldn't stand still, I couldn't look her in the eye, my heartbeat was going hard in my ear.

Mom kept her cool though. She didn't look surprised, she held the case far away from her like she was holding onto a dead rat.

Mom popped open the case, the weight and the dent in her skin where her wedding ring used to be.

They came, week by week, one week at a time, and then the rest came all at once, Mom opened up that case to the last eight tapes I had to hide. Eight tapes all lined up and wrapped in plastic.

Mom's face, the corner of her blood red eyes, a little bit of gray to her skin, and when she talked with her cigarette in her mouth, it sounded like she was talking through a straw.

"There are eight tapes here," she said, "8 through 16 where's 1 through 7?" I couldn't see her eyes, they were half closed, half awake.

Mom was figuring it out. I knew what was going to happen, but I had to stand there and wait. She took a long drag off her smoke, and held the case with her other hand.

Then she looked over at me, like I was the answer to the questions she was trying to figure out. There was a jump in her that went from her arm to her chest. She woke up real quick.

That muscle of anger, it spoke, in a voice deeper than normal. Her face kind of half lit up, awake from whatever sleep she was going through.

She leaned down to the coffee table, half tidy of Dad's things, and the chaos of mom, for a lighter. She lit up even though Dad forbade it.

"You've been hiding them from me." She said.

I knew that from the moment Dad put his hands on my shoulders, I knew it down in the garage. I knew it in all the ways that I hid the tapes, I knew Dad surprising Mom with a move to a different city was no kind of surprise at all.

"It was supposed to be a surprise," I said.

I'd played it so cool up until then, but now I'd really fucked the whole thing up. "What was supposed to be a surprise?" She said, "Why is he learning Spanish?" Mom was holding onto a vocabulary builder book, flipping through it, "Why is there so much ham she said?" she said, "What is he up to?"

Now was my chance to let her know this whole Miami thing was going to take care of all of us, not just Me and Dad. And that this thing I was hiding was a good thing.

"He's got a plan." I said, "The three of us are going to be rich." "What does that have to do with learning Spanish?"

"Miami," I said.

"What about Miami?" The empty in Mom's face was all the things she didn't know.

Miami was a different place when Mom said "Miami" not drawn out and dreamy like Dad said it. Mom said it like her tongue was a butcher's knife cutting up palm trees and sunshine.

Mom, it was hard to tell, but she had this crooked end of a half-smile on the edge of her lips.

"I think you better tell me the rest," she said.

So I laid down the whole story: me and Dad and Mom, Miami, swimming pools and ham sandwiches.

And after I'd laid out the whole story of me and Dad, Mom, and Miami, and why he needed to learn Spanish. I thought the story would free me from blame, but it didn't.

Mom's eyes didn't look at me the way she did the day she painted me, there was a brightness to her eyes that had fallen back asleep, and now they were focused on something else.

"What did he do, promise you sunshine and swimming pools?"

Then her face, her nose, her eyes, the half-asleep person left and in her place came this red-faced, red-haired demon woman with spit coming out of her mouth.

"You want to know what his plan is?" Mom said, "He's leaving me, and so are you."

My world got a whole lot smaller in that moment, a feeling I used to get when I would ride the rollercoaster at the county fair each Summer. All the other kids there loved the coaster, and I was terrified, I'd cry while I was on it. It was all that up and down, how my whole throw up stomach situation was because I felt like my life was like that, the sudden ups and downs, the spins and turns, gravity had its way with me. Then I saw it all for what it was, what it actually was, Dad's whole vision of what Miami was for us. Notably that there was no us in that equation, I was not a factor. There was no plan for me, It was all for him. I had this talk with Mom, so Dad didn't have to. I was Dad's escape route. "No, Mom, he said you were coming too, he said you could still paint in Miami."

Mom did this thing where she wouldn't look at me, only straight down at the floor down by my foot that wouldn't sit still. She did it when I did something so bad it couldn't be undone. "You love him too much, Jay" she said, "More than he deserves."

"Why would I want to leave now?" she said, she was getting so irritated, figuring it out, her hands up and down. "With everything that's just happened, when I'm so close to my dream coming true."

What I wanted then was the version of Mom who used to teach me to cook on cold winter nights, when Mom warmed up our two-story walk up with her spaghetti. Who lifted me up and let me stir the bubbling sauce. Who taught me how to chop an onion, and how you can mash garlic with the wide end of a butcher knife. I didn't know it then, but me hiding the tapes was me figuring Mom out, even if I didn't know it. Each week since the day she painted me, that Mom was replaced by a Mom who slept in all day, and went out every night.

When I was around the house she was either gone or I had to be super quiet all the time because she was asleep. Even when Mom was around and awake, it was like she was still asleep.

Mom in the seven weeks I hid the tapes. She wasn't a Mom, she was someone I didn't recognize. I didn't want to live with a mom like that.

But I didn't know how to ask for something I didn't understand.

So I stood there and stared at her red pink skin, the space above her chest. At all that mad on her face. Her face, her shoulders down at the floor of our porch, I couldn't even look her in the eye.

Somewhere in my head I think I always knew just how hard I worked to hide all seven of those tapes. Those tapes, all that hiding was for Dad. I didn't think about Mom at all.

Mom and I never talked about who knew what when. She knew I'd made the decision, only after she knew there was a reason for Dad and me to move away in the first place.

But back then I didn't piece together what I'd done until I'd done it, I'd chosen him over her.

Bella Vista

MOM AND THE MIRROR

CAME HOME ONE DAY and our front door was open and, when I got close enough, I heard the crunching guitars and a snarling English accent going on about saving some queen.

The music was so loud when I got up the front stairs, I had to plug up my ears with my fingers.

In the doorway were blue and pink curls of ribbon, horns and party hats, empty champagne bottles, but no people. The front door was open and anyone could just walk in. With all that noise, there was nobody in the living room, nobody over by Dad's bar, no one in the kitchen. There was smoke in the air, filled up ashtrays and tube-shaped glasses with little bits of champagne in them.

And next to all this on the living room coffee table was a magazine folded open to the middle. I had to make sure I was seeing it right, the window I looked out of that day in Mom's studio was right in the center of the magazine. The art books and paint cans and tea cups on Mom's desk, right next to the three paneled triptych. The one with the edges of my curly hair stretched out across three panels. The only painting Mom made of me was right in the center of the magazine.

There were words above the triptych that said *Kate Pershall, Center of the Universe*. This was an art magazine, and not just any art magazine. The one Mom subscribed to. Artforum.

Mom, she was famous, and I was famous too.

AND BACK THEN, I MIGHT'VE been young, but I was old enough to think it wasn't just Mom's party. This was the painting of the only time Mom really saw me, it was my party just as much as it was hers.

Upstairs there were voices that sounded like they came from inside a bottle.

UPSTAIRS IN MOM'S ROOM THE door was open, but the only thing there was the tangled mess of Mom's sheets, balled up and twisted.

From up in the studio, a cackle that could only be Mom's laugh.

I'M NOT UP THE STAIRS yet and already I know how they'll greet me, with hugs, and cake, they'll probably have cake and ice cream and let me drink coffee. My hand on the railing was shaking I was so excited.

Mom's voice from up there, "Who's up for more," Mom said, "let's do it all."

I WAS HALFWAY UP THE STAIRS and there was something off about her voice. My stomach pulled at me. It was Mom's big day and the way her voice sounded to me then, like she was too tired to celebrate.

I made it up to the top step, the open door to Mom's studio. Right away I couldn't see any cake anywhere, no cake, no ice cream. What I saw was a tall guy standing in the doorway, with long blue jeans, and a dirty white t-shirt with the sleeves torn off. His head was totally shaved with a big streak of pink hair down the middle all pointed up and spiky. This guy had these wraparound black sunglasses on. He was staring at one of Mom's empty canvases. The rest of Mom's studio, her unfinished canvases, empty easels, air brushes with dried paint on them, and ashtrays so full they spilled out onto mom's desk.

There was a ton of booze, vinyl records out in stacks, and people, Mom's studio was filled with people, weirdos like the man with long blonde hair and a bright orange blouse who looked like a woman, a man and a woman dressed all in black sat down on the floor, kissing like they do in the movies, arms and legs all sprawled out so I couldn't tell whose arm is whose.

There was one woman who wore all brown, even her glasses were brown, and she looked like an owl. Pretty sure she was the only one who saw me.

The pink mohawk came up from behind me, put the tips of his fingers on my shoulder when he scooched by me. He had a shirt on with three mean-looking guys on it and, in words that were bleeding, *The Clash*.

Mom's sleepy voice behind the guy with the Clash shirt. I couldn't see her.

I PUSHED PAST AND BUMPED MY nose into the purse of the owlish woman with blue sun glasses. She didn't say excuse me. All these people were standing around in a circle, except for the couple that were making out. They'd stopped kissing and were holding hands and looking over at a place I couldn't see. And I turned around towards the side of the studio with the high up window I looked through the day Mom painted me. I turned around and there she was, down on the ground. On her knees, Mom in her black going-out dress. Hair down across her face, kneeling down and moving like she was on a planet where gravity was different. She had a rolled-up dollar bill in her hand, her nervous hand was shaking.

Right in the middle of her party, with people all around, I walked up to her. I was standing just above her, close enough to touch.

"Mom," I said, "I saw the magazine. I'm so happy for you."

Book One 1980 | Mom And The Mirror

Mom heard me. I knew she heard me. I was right there in front of her, and she didn't lift up her head to see me. Her eyes didn't see me, she was so focused on her dollar bill.

People and space, bodies and shoulders and backs and belts. Seven bodies passing a square mirror with four lines of white powder. Three people on each side, and Mom in the middle. Mom, there was a pale to her, not just her face, but on her arms, her hand, and her fingers that held up the rolled-up dollar bill to her nose.

Mom might not have seen me, but the people did, they saw me and they saw what she was doing. They sat there and waited their turn.

"Kate," Pink Mohawk said, a voice in the middle of bodies and talk I couldn't understand words that meant something only to artists. Art words. "Your kid is up here."

But Mom didn't hear or didn't respond.

Mom inhaled those lines like it was the most important thing she'd ever done.

Mom down on her knees breathed in with her nose, each of those lines of powder were erased by the dollar bill.

Mom's voice called out to me like I wasn't just in front of her.

"Not now, Jay," she said, "Mama's working" her eyes went down to the empty mirror.

PINK MOHAWK WALKED UP TO me, put his hand on my shoulder, burst of warmth through my chest. His eyes were red fire bloodshot. He might have looked tough, but his voice had this whisper to it, like he was doing something he wasn't supposed to.

"Sorry kid," he said. "You gotta go downstairs."

THE WAY HE STOOD, IF I moved left, he moved right, if I tried to turn around and see where Mom was, he blocked me. I tried to get a good look at Mom. Then Pink Mohawk put his body in my way.

"You shouldn't see your Mom like this,"

"**W**HO THE FUCK LET HIM up here?" Mom said, her eyes were black and closed off.

And there's one of those moments that I'll remember forever. Mom there with those closed off black eyes of hers. Mom, her face, the eyes, they don't look almost blue and they don't look almost green, they wasn't any hazel color in those eyes, no room for any seeing of any kind, just life going on in front of her with nothing to paint. More wrinkles around her face than I'd ever seen, it looked like Mom had painted a portrait of the person that made her sleepy all the time.

The person who never saw the sun, who slept all day, who stuck dollar bills up their noses and had people over for a party, her party, not mine.

Book One 1980 | Mom And The Mirror

The picture of the person who was supposed to be my mother, those black-on-black eyes and wrinkles around her eyes. Pale skin because she never went outside anymore.

I ran as fast as I could down those stairs to Mom and Dad's room, by the bed with the pictures of us as a family.

I barely made it to their bathroom. The smell of cold water when it's surrounded by porcelain, hot red pulp of fruit punch burning all the way up my throat and into the bowl.

I threw up like all of who I was came out of me, and I kept on throwing up until I slid off and laid down on the bathroom floor. On the ceiling the music was coming down from Mom's studio. Half sounds of words and laughs, muffled voices from upstairs, and somewhere in the middle of all that noise was Mom's voice.

But I didn't see her, couldn't make out her voice from the other voices. Upstairs they were dancing, they carried on with their party.

Down here I put my hand on the side of the toilet and it felt as cool and sweaty as my hand. The lid was up and there were Mom's long red hairs on the lid, those hairs of hers got into every room in the house.

No music from upstairs, just the sound of the toilet filling up. Mom's voice coming through the ceiling. I couldn't hear what she said, I felt the edges of her words from her voice in my body, I knew what it meant in the pale skin of my arms and chest.

Someone was coming downstairs from the studio. Sounded like the kind of shoes Mom wore on her disco nights. Mom was coming down to say goodnight, that at the end she loved me no matter what.

And the door opened and I closed my eyes, because it was Mom and I still loved Mom, and the door opened, and there was no disco night outfit, there was Pink Mohawk with his bleeding Clash shirt, and his sunglasses.

He stood by the door, and he saw me there, and he came over to me, and I didn't know what he was going to do but he crouched down, got his knee down on the floor, the knee that was showing from the ripped-up hole in his jeans, and he reached out and put his hand on my head and rubbed it the way Dad used to. He looked around at the puke in the toilet, at me and how I looked. He didn't say a word, he didn't run away, he got some tissue and wiped my chin, and held out his hand to me, with the skull ring.

And he took one hand and pulled his glasses off, real slow. He didn't look scary with his glasses off, brown eyes the same color as mine. He didn't look like he'd ever done this before. He looked much younger, this guy, this kid, he could've been my older brother. With his hand on my shoulder, he felt around for my muscles and bones and pulled me closer to him. He smelled like cigarettes and some kind of sweet other people's body odor I'd never smelled before.

I closed my eyes, I didn't know what was going to happen next. I closed my eyes so I didn't have to see those Clash guys on his bleeding shirt.

I moved my head over to where his knee was and he sat down and slid his feet down on the ground and he pulled me towards him and grabbed my chin with his fingers and looked me dead in the eye. Here, for now, I was safe.

Pink Mohawk and his big blood-red eyes, going back and forth slow. Taking the whole situation in. He put his long finger under my chin and pushed it up and he looked me right in the eye and wasn't in a hurry. And what he said he said twice to make sure I heard it.

"I'm sorry buddy," he said. "I really am."

AND I DON'T KNOW WHY, but in a way, it was like that guy with the pink mohawk was a parent to me then, more than any of my own parents were. Dad with all of his high and mighty bullshit, it took a guy with a mohawk and a Clash T Shirt to put his son to bed, to wipe his forehead when he got sick, to hold him, to be there.

Right there, in his arms as I fell asleep, I knew it in my body if it wasn't in my head yet. All of what happened, I'd never go back, and things had gone too far in one direction for that, sooner or later, it had to snap back.

Bella Vista

RISE AND SHINE

MORNING WAS A BRIGHT light in my eyes at I didn't know what time. I was 12 years old, I just about knew that much.

I woke up on the couch in the main room. I was in my underwear. My clothes weren't on the floor. A flash of last night with puke down the front of my shirt. and Pink Mohawk taking off my pukey clothes and tucking me in. The coffee table had a full ashtray and plastic party cups turned upside down. Didn't know what time I went to bed the night before. Or what time Pink Mohawk left, or where Mom was, or anyone for that matter. The house was quiet.

I got up and walked around, trying to figure out who was up and who was asleep. Dad was at work, of course. Through her studio door upstairs I could hear Mom snoring.

In my room, propped up on my desk was a greeting card with the state of Florida on it. On the inside was Dad's slanted handwriting:

> How 'bout we start a new life? Forever your Pal
> —Dad

It wasn't exactly subtle.

It all seemed really sudden, and then I remembered how last night Dad came home super late and he was talking to me like I was as awake as he was, but I was asleep in my underwear and Dad kept talking and I don't remember half of what Dad told me. I told him I loved him and his plan, and was happy to be a part, and I fell back asleep.

I was tired, so tired I was barely aware I was sleeping on the couch in my underwear. I tried to imagine what Pink Mohawk did with my laundry.

I had to think about something else, I didn't want to think about Mom and how she chose those lines of white powder over me.

Late at night, with the comforter down over me, on the couch, half-dreaming our conversation. I must've told Dad about it because the whole we're-going-to-leave thing got jumped up by a month.

I've always been a heavy sleeper.

There was no one to take me to school, so I climbed into my bed. Took a little inventory before I fell asleep: My posters, my record player, my Mazinga.

𝔍**T WAS DARK WHEN I** woke up again, to the sound of the front door closing. Dad and the same steps in the door, every goddamned evening, the clink of two ice cubes into his glass of bourbon. I walked out to the landing.

"He's alive," Dad said. There was something about the way he stood there, not pushed down by some external force, he stood straight up, his tie was loose around his neck. He threw his blazer onto the couch and let it sit there.

"Quit my job today," he said. Swear to god he rubbed his hands together. Picked up the bourbon on the coffee table, took a big swig.

"This Miami thing is a go."

Dad stuck out a finger at me, turned it into a gun, made a little pow pow sound.

"All thanks to you, big guy," he said.

𝔗**HE THING WITH MOM CRASHING** like it did, and the reason why I was pretty sure it sure had to do with me, that I fucked up the whole tapes thing, so after that, I was kind of dead to her, but she couldn't do that when she was straight that's why she did it when she did it.

There was so much I didn't know then as a twelve year old, but for the old guy I am now, I have things I have to say the things I only just last week figured out.

Bella Vista

GOODBYE

I **WAS STANDING UPSTAIRS IN** front of the closed door of Mom's studio on our last day in Park Slope when I realized what I'd gotten myself into.

When Dad first talked me into this whole Miami thing, he did so with palm trees and warm sun, a swimming pool, and a tennis court. But now that I was here, now that it was me telling Mom we were going to leave, I felt different about it.

After all that had happened with Mom, I knew that something had to change. She wasn't fit to be a mother, she needed time alone, and hopefully the person who she was when she was on her knees the other night would pass if we gave her the space she needed. And now that she did what she did at her party, now my hand was dealt.

I had the card, the only thing for me to do now was to play it.

LIFE WAS MOVING SO FAST. Back then it seemed like one minute I was throwing up in the toilet with Pink Mohawk taking care of me, and two days later Dad and I were leaving.

As for my role in this, my handling or mishandling of the tapes I was supposed to hide, Dad never said anything about me getting caught. None of that mattered by that point. I like to think that whatever Dad was trying to hide was going to come out one way or another.

Mom and Dad were never going to work.

BUT THAT DIDN'T MEAN IT was easy for me to say goodbye. The door to Mom's studio shut, the smoke from the cigarette she was smoking in there gave my nose a tickle. The music from inside sounded like a punk act that had mellowed into disco.

A small knock wasn't going to do it. I needed to pound, and I needed to pound hard.

When she did finally come to the door Mom was dressed head to toe in black, her hair all done up.

"Let's make this quick" she said. "I got an opening I'm already late to."

She dropped her hand and walked back to what she was doing, getting ready to go out, putting on her makeup, her eyeliner, the whole thing.

In her studio there were no empty canvases with half-finished work, no finished ones hanging from invisible wires. No canvases at all. Only empty wine and cocktail glasses. A party stopped and not picked back up again.

I sat down on the stool across from her desk. The two of us on either side of each other, like before, but different.

Me there on that last day, I wanted the version of Mom who painted me, but she was too gone for that. Dad did what he did and I did what I did and now we were fucked.

She looked over at me, with this half smile that made fun of the kind of people Dad was, people who charged people for everything by the hour.

"So whatcha got to say to me, kid, time is money."

I slid a little on the stool, I'd grown a lot since I was last on it. "I came to say goodbye," I said.

MOM DIDN'T IGNORE ME LIKE she did the night before. She put down her pocket mirror and her mascara pencil. She got up and came over to where I was on the stool. She leaned over, got her arms around me, the bangs of her flowing red hair on my cheek. Mom, and the trace of perfume, and the clean clinical smell of vodka.

I didn't have words for what she did with those three little lines on the mirror, even if I kept telling myself that she deserved to be left behind, I couldn't really believe it.

"We're leaving tomorrow," I said.

SHE STAYED THERE IN MY arms. She couldn't speak. She couldn't move. We sat there for awhile like that, in the window on the ceiling, the skylight, there weren't any leaves on any branches anywhere.

Me and Mom on the stool, holding on.

"YOU WILL BE OK," SHE said to me. "Even if he does what I think he's going to do, at least you'll be rich."

Mom right there, her chest against my chest. Mom, the thing between us, the connection we still hadn't been, burned up.

I felt it then, the way she broke when I was holding her. A shake back there, Mom took a breath in. Mom was crying. She wanted it hidden, she didn't want me to know she felt anything.

"I'm sorry," Mom said in a voice as sad as everything and just as far away. Her eyes weren't cloudy or distant, they were raw red from crying.

All the Mom of the last few months wasn't there anymore, it was the old Mom again, the one who fought for what she wanted.

She slipped her index finger on my neck, raised it up and lifted my chin so I could look her right in the eye.

"You are your own man," she said, "never forget that."

She looked down at the table. It would be just me for a while, me and him, me and Dad.

It was always the plan, but now it really hit me.

Mom did the thing I never thought she could do, she came through and with the slow movement of her two lips, and that was the only way she could really tell me. She mouthed the words, she got the closest anyone can get to saying it out loud but not saying it. What she said was what most mothers say all the time, but from her, that was the first time she used her lips to say it.

I love you: Is what her lips said, and when I looked at her, into her eyes, they didn't want me to go, her eyes wanted me to stay.

Bella Vista

EXORCISM

I **WAS UP HALF THE** night, imagining that everything from the painting in MOMA to the tapes had happened to someone else, a bad movie on TV.

In between my thoughts, I heard Mom heard her up in her studio. The zipping sound in the night of her duffel bag. It was late when I finally woke up, a sunny haze out of my window, quiet with the occasional honk in the middle of a weekday morning.

Dad was on the other bed in the room, the weight of his hand on my shoulder, I thought I was dreaming when Dad woke me up, I thought it was one of his old photos mixed up in my dreams, but there he was when I sat up in bed, Dad and his clean-shaven face, no beard. Dad and his fresh-from-the-barber's haircut from the day before.

The evolution of my Dad went with his hairstyle, from the long, greasy days of the Karmann Ghia, to the not-quite-an-afro beard style for the air conditioning factory, to this trimmed down version that sat in front of me. Dad changed his look with what he wanted out of life.

Dad had become so careful in making his decisions, it's amazing he'd ever been carefree enough to be too stoned to drive home. Even when Dad had three or four bourbons, it was just enough to shrink the tension in the room.

The more I woke up that morning, the more dad changed.

Went over to the door with the coat in his arm, then he put it on, Dad, a vision in Sky Blue, Dad was wearing a suit with success woven right into the fibers, the same sky-blue thread that his dress shirt was made out of, the color of a social climber. His suit might've been calling the shots, but his lips and his boxer nose weren't saying anything until the deal was done.

Dad told me to pack a few things. I took the portrait of me as a series of bicycle spokes. I crammed a few X-Men comics inside my backpack. I was getting too old for dolls, sword or no sword..

Dad didn't take anything. He left behind all of his clothes, all the records from the Dirty Hippie days. All he brought with him was his car keys, and the plastic suitcase with the tapes. Walking out, I tried to find one last relic of my mother. The only thing in her studio was a canvas with one long looping line on a rickety easel I found on the floor by the trashcan. The rest of the room was just empty walls, empty drawers, empty closets and empty cabinets. After I had fallen asleep she went from room to room, and cleared everything out.

Reading mom was as unscientific as my inability to read the tea leaves in her mug when she painted me. I spent years just waiting for one of those little tea chunks to float up to the surface.

All the love I have for my Mother got ground down in my chest where the I'm-going-to-puke-feeling was.

Maybe what I wanted from her just wasn't what she was. Maybe what I wanted was the kind of TV Mom who would do whatever it took to see that her son was safe.

And then, in the bathroom, I saw it, the last relic of Mom, the long looping line of Mom's wedding ring, the same kind of line she left behind on the lone canvas of her studio.

Mom's ring, the weight of it in my hand, all the past of Mom and Dad concentrated into six ounces. I slipped it into my pocket, and we were out of there.

Bella Vista

START YOUR ENGINES

FOR MY TENTH BIRTHDAY, I got a two-day, twenty-six-hour road trip that started in Park Slope in Brooklyn and ended in the salty air of Miami, and most of it was spent sitting on the soft fabric in the back of Dad's car.

All Dad talked about on the way down was his new business. He said that even though the deal was still not done, he said there was all this money floating around us, and all we had to do was grab it. He told me this after all the phone stops we made on the way down to Miami, another rest stop, another pay phone. With all of this, there was so much new for me to be excited about, but all I could think of was Mom.

Mom and I the night before, for just a second I felt like one of her paintings, the only thing that mattered.

And just as soon as the painting feeling came, it got washed away. After she told me she loved me, her big I'm-proud-of-you smile changed back into the empty eyes of Mom on drugs.

With each mile we drove farther from the outlines of the Manhattan skyline, the more Mom faded into that last bright spring morning, burning everything around it, and through it all was the continuous burn of road and the snap of stop and start on Dad's in-dash cassette player, "Hola, me llamo es." The tape said.

We listened to the basic subject verb agreement tape, the vocabulary builder tape, and the conversational starter tape, but it wasn't until after we cleared the last of the Jersey Turnpike, when Dad puts something else in.

FINDING THE WOUNDED ANIMAL WITHIN it's called. The narrator told us that whatever painful event that had recently happened to the listener could be easily overcome, if he could find the strength inside. But in order to do that, he had to address the pain inside of him, what the voice on the tape called the "Wounded Animal Within." With a little nurturing and a lot of what the guy called "Personal Empowerment," anyone could turn their wounded animal into a power animal.

The voice said each of us had one, said we had to find ours.

DAD'S FACE WAS IN BETWEEN the driver and passenger seats. He turned around and flashed his smile at me for a second.

"So what's your power animal," He asked.

My HANDS WERE NUMB FROM sitting on them for so long.

My fingernails are chewed down to the nubs of red and sore. All the things I needed but didn't know how to ask, or say.

Dad sees me looking at my hands in the rear view mirror. "You're probably more of an ostrich," he said.

We drove into the disappearing skyline to the flat nowhere of Delaware, down toward the swollen bulb of Maryland. I let my mind stretch out and grow heavy with vocabulary builders and power animals. I fell into the trance of a dozy nap.

We finally stopped driving in Virginia.

We PULLED INTO THE FIRST Best Western we saw on the highway. Dad got us a two-room suite. I was cold in the shorts I was wearing when we checked in the late afternoon, got our bags loaded from the car, found the room, went through the lobby that smelled of fresh linens and chlorine, and beyond the lounge, above the pool and the soda machines, past open doors of rooms that were all decorated the same, one more flight of stairs up to the suite, one large master bedroom, one side room, in between a couch and a TV. And as soon as I got settled in, got my teeth brushed, Dad came out of the bathroom, fresh shirt, tie and slacks.

"I've got to go out for a bit," Dad said, "Phone calls, investors. This deal is so close. You can call room service."

Dad and his leaving. I should have seen it as the pattern it would become, how the only thing I could rely on with Dad was for him to leave. But it was the first time, the first time in a series of "I don't have the time."

At least I could call room service, we never had that kind of money until then.

Sitting up in that bed in my room, at twelve years old, with a scratchy comforter, sheets and pillow, I felt like I was completely replaceable, that there were a thousand versions in this building in a motel where all the rooms looked the same. I was a nobody in a motel without personality, far from the triptychs and long flowing lines that Mom drew, far from Pink Mohawk, and all the other things I thought I'd never miss about her, but alone in this strange hotel room, I got it: Mom's desire to stand out. To be different, to be heard.

I saw it looking around the room, at the pink and pistachio sailboat painting, one of any number of pink and pistachio paintings, and how many of them there were in this hallway, all decorated the same, the same peach-spackle walls and curtains all the way down the hallway. Dozens of rooms lined up like, coffins and if you wanted to be remembered, then a Best Western in the middle of bumfuck Virginia just off the highway was not the place to be.

That said. The TV. The room service, all the things I was about the receive, I had no idea what was about to happen next. Full of dread one second, then excited about swimming pools, our Bella Vista, the next.

Turned on the TV just in time to catch *Conan, The Barbarian*, the part where James Earl Jones telekinetically controlled the serpents, this hotel room, I wanted all the snakes in wherever we were to rise up and take me out of here.

I called room service, and the whole ordeal took the rest of the Conan movie before a guy in a cheap, white tuxedo knocked on the door. The burger I ordered was covered in this round metal tin, with a whole other tin that had fries in it. And a milkshake that was regular milk mixed with a scoop of chocolate ice cream that had almost melted.

The fries were cold and the burger tasted burnt, from the first bite to the third bite where I finally laid it down on the tray in front of me.

I slid the tray off my lap, I got up and grabbed the creases in the curtains, the emptiness behind them, just shadows and the roar of the road.

In this anonymous room, with the decor the exact same as all the others on this floor, I could be anywhere in America, I wanted to see the outside world to know I was still in the land of the living. I wanted to know that leaving Mom behind didn't send me into a well-ordered coffin the same design as all the others. I pulled the curtains back to see who I was based on where we were.

And on this day my view was of the back alley of a hotel, a green and brown dumpster, with rows of trees behind before the highway that took over the view, the browned-out edges of leaves next to distant cars going over a river, in between states.

And sitting there, in front of the dumpster, was a tiny black kitten. And even though it was getting dark, and even though our room was on the 2nd floor, I could still see this kitten. It's green eyes reflected back at me. This cat had been almost eaten away by fleas and god knows what else. It was meowing at whoever happened to be looking. It could've been me who saved it. I could've run out there and held its boney body, felt that heartbeat fast in my arms, the little skeletal frame around it.

I COULD'VE LOOKED UP AT THE way the highway was a stage and the trees around it were its curtain, with a bridge almost disappearing over the horizon line, but the cat saw me, because it arced its head up at me, and I couldn't look at that thing and his mouth making meowing sounds any longer. I closed the curtain and called room service about the burger.

"That's our charbuger." the lady on the phone said. "It's delicious."

IT WAS LATE WHEN I woke up, to the charburger on a plate next to me in bed. Dad and the sounds of someone else in the living room area of our suite.

"It's a good thing we went to your place," Dad said.

A WOMAN'S VOICE SAID. "WELL, WE couldn't do it here."

"You want me to talk to him?" the woman said.

"WHY WOULD YOU WANT TO do that?" Dad said. As if there was ever a time that I needed someone. Tonight was it.

"He just lost his mom"

"It's not like she died," Dad said. "She was a horrible role model."

Boom! There it was. The sweet sugary middle of dad's plan. The trick I fell for.

I CLOSED MY EYES, TRIED TO listen to anything but the two of them, their footsteps into the master bedroom, the door closing, the faint sound of the electrical current running through the walls, sounds of the highway and cars and rain outside.

How many of them danced across my wall before I fell asleep. Fifteen twenty roars until I heard Dad come in with some strange woman.

We were only one day away and already he was kissing and whatever else made those sounds I didn't want to think about.

The whispering and the bumps against the door. Eighteen wheelers bombing down the highway in the middle of the night.

Bella Vista

FLORIDA

IT WASN'T UNTIL WE were couple of hours north of Orlando when we started to see the strange otherness of Florida in full view. The first clues were in the road signs, like the one for Weeki Wachee, that said *Live Mermaids* with a real picture of four women in a pyramid, women underwater with mermaid suits blowing bubbles. The sign hadn't been updated from the sixties.

The little row houses we passed on the highway went from Southern white picket fences to more pastel colors the further south we drove. What Dad used to say how, "the road to hell being paved with houses in various shades of pastel colors." At first there were only a few of these houses, but by the time we got down to Palm Beach every other house could be mistaken for a retiree's pant leg.

And it was there, just south of Fort Lauderdale, when that salty marsh air hit us, that wall of humidity.

And here was where I started to feel like the air was being cut off from me, slow so I wouldn't notice. Not full breaths, like in New York, whenever I breathed, for as long as I was south of Fort Lauderdale, my breathing would be restricted, it would be that way until I died or I left, whatever came first.

Dad's world, his new house, this new world, this wasn't my world. It was his.

My finger was on the little rise of the window button. I rolled it down enough to let a big mouthful of marsh air in. The smell-it-once-and-you'll-never-forget-it air. This salty smell, like if you covered the entire southern tip, was a salty marsh because it is, and it will always smell that way, as long as it's above water.

We weren't even there yet, and already it felt like a reset. We wouldn't be the same people we were in Park Slope, down here we'd change, we'd become better people. I felt like I did that day in the car with Dad as the Dirty Hippie, when he told me this, the car, the roads, everything, was for me. We weren't there yet, and I couldn't quite breathe properly, but apart from that, I was having the time of my life.

REFUGEE

WE HAD THE WINDOWS rolled down. It was hot, slow and sticky. My head was out the window. I was trying to find patches of Miami blue water Dad promised me.

Miami, we had arrived.

I didn't have anything to compare this new place to. It felt like the rules of gravity were different here. Things looked closer together.

There were billboards by the highway, so much closer than they were in New York. It was like they were right on top pressing down on the cars. Signs for cigarettes, for rum, a guy all suited up in pads for Jai Alai. Half the street names were in Spanish, so I recognized the letters, but they were in the wrong places.

Then off to the right, I saw this shadow underneath the highway, so much gray and white, and then this thing so quick and so dark it shook me out of my daydream. I couldn't even tell what it was back then, but somewhere inside of me was someone who was aware that in that tent slept dozens of people, maybe even a hundred in this one big green rectangle underneath the highway overpass.

I was scared but I had to get Dad's attention. I did something I never did. I took my hand that was in my lap and lifted it up.

I reached out my hand. Pointed my index finger. His knuckle on the steering wheel, my finger touched the spot on his finger where his wedding band used to be. Ten fingers, and I had to touch the one without the ring.

"Pull over," I said.

I don't think I'd ever said anything that demanding in my whole life.

HE WOULDN'T HAVE LISTENED, WOULD have wanted things done his way, but Dad pulled over so fast and with no questions asked. Maybe he felt sorry for me, he probably figured, "I can do this, I can pull over for him, he deserves it."

He pulled the car over into this extra half a lane on the bridge that was there in case someone got a flat tire.

I got out, left the door open, and this "Ping" sounded the car. Dad stayed in there, writing down the mileage in his book, totally unfazed.

I ran over to the edge of the railing, and there it was, a few feet away, the spot where I could see what this thing was. Right there, close enough to really see it, a big wide rectangle, army-issued green, there were four steel ties on each corner. This rectangle was a huge tent. There was a salt bite to the air, the sound of seagull cries bounced off concrete walls.

THE TENT DOWN THERE WAS closer than before. There were rows of cots, support cables tied down, and sandbagged. People sitting on cots, scratching their heads, drinking water from a large cooler.

There was a group of men hanging out at one end of the tent. They were standing around smoking. Of course, I couldn't hear what they were saying, I was too far away. There were about five of them, but one stood out to me. He was wearing this black all-in-one mechanic's jumper.

He was the only one with a smile on his face. He had what looked to me at the time like a scrabbly start to a beard, and he looked right up toward where I was looking from, right at me.

These people, standing around big water coolers, pitchers, pots and pans, the smell of cooked onions, they weren't just hanging out, they weren't camping, these people didn't have anywhere else to go, these people lived underneath the highway.

There was a fence a few feet in front of the tent, tall enough for three or four people tall. And at the top when you got there, if you managed to get there, there was this spiky stuff knotted in clumps placed along the top of the fence. Razor wire.

There were people living underneath the highway, not in a history book, but right in front of me. This whole people-living-under-the-highway-thing, I know now they were Cuban refugees. I know they were kicked out of Cuba, but I didn't know the whole deal yet. Sure, I heard people on the radio talking about it, but they were talking about it like the people who got kicked out weren't people at all, they called them all kinds of names, they called them "criminals." To me, it was horrible these people were new to this country and already they were guilty.

There were tents with hundreds of these people living under overpasses all over Miami, but there was this one guy standing around smoking. He looked up at where I was, his friends or whatever were pointing at me. He is the only one who's stood up straight. He's the only one who had a smile on his face. He saw me, the sides of his mouth got wider, because he was already smiling but now he opened his mouth, a smile so big I could see his yellow teeth, that black mechanic jumpsuit with a white patch, and sewn in dark blue stitching was his name. I couldn't make out the whole name, it was too far for that, but I could make out a J and an A.

This man, his smile, in the middle of a tent city, he had something to smile about. I wish I could protect him, to do all the things the US couldn't. I wanted to take care of him the way no one stepped up and took care of me. I wanted to run down there and get close enough to talk to him, to really take in that smile on his face. He smiled at me like I was the first kid he'd seen in America.

From where I stood his body was about the size of one of the action figures I used to play with back in Park Slope. His voice, when he spoke to me, sounded like he was a little drunk, but maybe he was just pretending to be. A little pretend drunk sing song. He was far away but me but I still heard it, so he must've yelled.

"Hola chico, que tal," he said. "Hace buen dia."

HE STUCK HIS HAND UP, took his pinky and this thumb and made this bird shape with his hand, twisted it around so I could see it there, the dark green of the tent, the steel of the cots, then this guy smiling and singing out to me like he wasn't sure I was there at all, like I was some kind of hallucination, a version of his son in Havana he was seeing in Miami.

I wanted to wave back. But Dad never let me get that far. Dad's hand down on the part of my shoulder he used to stop me cold in my tracks, gave me a squeeze to let me know I wasn't going anywhere.

"Down there," he said. "You want to go down there?"

Dad's eyes, both of them were on me, not so much cross eyed as cross haired.

I had no time to put together thoughts that would even form an argument, no time to say what was on my mind. So it was just him answering these big questions for me.

"He looked nice," I said, his face, the way his smile came off his face, his eyes and how there was love in the way they hung there on his face.

"You think they need your pity?" Dad said.

"**W**HAT THIS GUY WON'T TELL you is he is a criminal, all of these people are criminals. Castro emptied his prisons. These are criminals you are feeling sorry for."

My refugee down there called out to me, but he couldn't see me. "Chico, chico de güero," he said, "¿Donde esta tuyo?"

Dad, his back straight, his perfect posture, his face dipped down to me, took his hand on my shoulder and pulled me into an almost hug.

"These people are Castro's trash."

WHAT DAD SAID HIT ME right in the stomach. I knew how it felt on my body, even if I didn't know what it meant. I needed to say something, so he would know, a clear statement of what I thought about my man.

"They're just people, Dad."

I THOUGHT HE WOULD BE MOVED by this or at least change his expression some, but he held me there, so close I could smell the cologne giving way to his sweat smell, smelled like old age. Dad didn't let go, he stood there, with his arm around me, he wasn't letting go, he was pulling me closer.

His two brown eyes, not open, rigid hard, right on me.

"Anyone who can't help themselves doesn't deserve to be helped," he said.

This belief Dad had, that only certain people deserved things, that there were people in this world that suffered.

I've learned since then that there were two kinds of people in this world, one who could be crushed at the sight of someone living underneath an overpass and the other was someone whose face never changed at the sight of them.

Dad turned his body around, facing back towards the car, his arm still around my shoulder, this was some kind of father son bonding moment to him, but behind me, I knew my refugee was still standing there, and I had to say goodbye, I had to tell him something.

I threw my body around, whip fast, a spin move I used during dodgeball. Spun my body around, and before Dad even knew what was what, I was tear ass out of there on a run six steps free of him. All I saw was that railing and that tent getting closer, and when I get to the railing My Refugee was still standing there, but not with his hand up or out. His smile was gone, but he was still looking up at that spot.

I held my hand up nice and tall so he could see it, so tall I had to get on my tiptoes to make sure he saw it.

I was headed to our new house on Bella Vista. On that night I'd lay my head down on my new waterbed, and this guy had to lay his head down on some barely-there pillow, in that sweaty bed with, like, fifty other people. I'd be in my air-conditioned house with my water bed, and he was in the middle of downtown Miami under an overpass.

He wouldn't be able to sleep because he had a family back in Havana, a wife and a kid. Me, I was just happy to have a pool.

"Hey Chico," the man said. "Bien suerte."

I didn't know it at the time, but what he said to me was Good luck. And I couldn't have known that from the words, but I must've felt something that he wanted me to feel.

I wanted him to know I was different, that I wasn't like Dad, the reason why I couldn't understand all that political talk on the radio was because at the end of the day this guy was just as much a person as me or Dad.

I raised up my hand nice and tall, so I could see him see me. And the words, it was the only Spanish I knew.

"Te quiero," I said.

What I said to him was "I love you." In Spanish.

AND DAD BEING DAD, JUST couldn't let me go. Right there behind me again, his breath on my neck, his thick hand on my shoulder, pressed down on the one pressure point that connects to the rest of my body, one grip and my body goes back to being under him.

"Let's go home," Dad said.

THIS MOMENT, DAD STILL HAD his hand down on my shoulder. Me telling him how I wanted to meet this man, go down there and get right up to the fence, close enough to where I could say hello and he'd be able to see what color my eyes were, but Dad felt so strong about this, about me needing protection, how I couldn't go down there on my own, felt so strongly about it he was willing to pull me down with his own hand.

Dad standing there forcing my hand, and me there, a bystander in my own life. And how one day I'd throw that hand off, I'd run down there and hug my refugee, unlock the gate and let him ride shotgun.

Bella Vista

ARRIVAL

DAD AND I WERE driving down Old Cutler Road on our way to Bella Vista Avenue. There were great old trees covering what we could see above us. I don't know if they were elk or elm, but I don't think there was a single patch of sky that wasn't covered by the looped-over branches of trees.

Dad had one hand on the wheel straight up at the top, his other hand on the seat behind me. A hug that never happened.

"Things are going to be better here," Dad said.

DAD'S EYES STILL HELD ONTO the promise of this Miami thing, that we could still change as people. He tipped his head down so I could see the brown in his eyes behind his glasses.

"I'm going to be a better father to you," he said.

His eyes, they were softer, not as intense, I figured maybe he was telling me the truth.

We DROVE BY VARIOUS HOUSES, one block, then two, then a left turn on this street that was split in two with a grassy tree-lined median strip run down the middle. On one side of the street were houses, in blocks. Funny thing was there was no normal green street signs. The street signs were made out of white cement and placed on the ground at intersections.

Mangroves are an ecosystem, made up of low-lying salt water. These curly brick red branches, and there was a whole system of the stuff right across the street. The combination of the branches and salt water makes a perfect feeding ground for birds and blue crab and these little prehistoric suction cup nightmares called horseshoe crabs. These mangroves didn't just smell bad, they made noises. In my kid head I heard the click and whirr of some sort of unknown creature across the street, plotting and scheming, always alive.

The other side of the street were mangroves, and the smell was so salty it could knock you out. A few more blocks down on the intersection, right past one of those round white cement street signs was our two storied glass panel revealing a staircase of a house, our house, Bella Vista.

Bella Vista, the arrival of Dad's dream, a half-moon driveway and a white wall that surrounded the place. There was the two-story part of the house that came up from behind the wall. There was a whole lot of something on the other side of the wall to the part of the house where the second story rose up out of the patio in a big pane of glass.

But once we pulled into the half-moon driveway, once I got out and heard the sound of water being shot through a plastic tube, that got rid of the we-live-across-the-street-from-a-jungle fears right then and there.

There was this little gate tucked into the wall. I couldn't see it when we first pulled in, I only saw it when I got close enough to the center of the little wall that wrapped around the front of the house, two steps and a gate, two steps that changed me.

Inside that wall was a Jacuzzi. The cover was off, the white frothy water was dancing, and above it was the bright green of the tennis court next to the house. Beyond that was the seawall, a concrete wall that boats pull up to.

To the left was the pool, this large rectangle with this alternating light/ dark blue water that looked to be about the most inviting I had ever seen. When I saw these things, this pool, this Jacuzzi, it took me a few minutes to see the rest of the house behind it, the house was set back, it let the Jacuzzi and the pool do the talking.

This window was a two-story tall piece of glass, where I could see inside to a set of carpeted stairs going from the bottom floor to the top. From marble tiled flooring on the ground floor to the carpet on the second floor. There was other stuff too, a long wide living room, but really I was all about the pool.

The blue water of the pool was a promise I could lie in, a big rectangle in the middle of all this stained, elegant patio tile.

And, yeah, I saw the rest of the ground floor of the house when I pulled my shirt off and put it down on a chair with this white mesh plastic fabric. The rest of the house went around the pool in a U-shape of windows that started with a room with a TV and a couch, then the breakfast nook of the kitchen, where I could watch cartoons and eat my cereal at the same time. The rest of the U carried on through the kitchen to the hallway, which led to the stairwell you could also see from the pool. The other side of the U ended up by the Jacuzzi, all of that was Dad's bedroom, but the blinds were drawn and I couldn't see anything in there.

I didn't even know what Dad was doing. I know he was talking and trying to give me some kind of tour from the patio, but I had my socks off, my shirt hung on the chair, my watch on the table next to it. I had my feet on the edge of the tile of a slightly darker color.

First Crack is what I called the first time I jump into any new water. I did it then and I still do it now. It's a sacred thing to me. I don't believe in anything anymore, but after all I've seen and done I still believe in First Crack.

You know the sound you make when you first jump into water, when it's been weeks or months since you've been under? The sound your body makes when it hits water, that's First Crack. We're talking about the moment I reached full submersion, when I was down there I entered a world where things move like they should all the time.

That pool, that day with the limestone and the chalky tile. First Crack was going back into the place that birthed me, and when I came up for air I was a new person.

Book One 1980 | Arrival

Me there, in my underwear, I got down to the bottom, on my back, my head up to the top and there was Dad's face, his cartoon face wiggling over the pool, and even though my eyes were stinging I had to hold them open to see Dad.

And I turned looked down at my feet to go and come back up, only I didn't even get that far because when put my feet down at the scratchy bottom to push up back to the surface, there was this light I saw coming from the bottom, this square bit of glass on the wall of the pool where the water was brighter than the rest. And I pushed forward, blew more air out of my nose to pull me closer, because I had to, this was the time, swim closer to that light, dear boy.

Because this part of my story is the part where I start to see just how much I have inside of me, that even something as slight as a light change, was to me world hearing what I had to say.

I didn't even make it down to where the light in the water changed color, because when I came back up for air, Dad was there talking to someone. This other guy had a limo drivers hat and a suit that was about two sizes too big for him. A tie loose around his neck, white shirt, black blazer with all these stains on it. His hair was tight and curly and he had bags under his eyes and a mustache that covered up whatever youth he might have had on his face.

He looked like he needed some sleep and definitely a shower.

"This is Cliff," Dad said.

My dad's face went from the usual frown of concentration to something lighter, someone younger before Dad gave a shit, back when he didn't take himself so serious.

These two, they grew up together, the way Dad and Cliff stood there on that first day, it wasn't about them standing, the way they stood close enough to be close, but enough space for the two to have an optimal view of the other.

When I started paying attention again, Cliff was talking about his limo business.

"It was a real boom time about four years ago. When all the old Jewish grannies started moving down here and they liked the way I talked to 'em, so I had enough dough and enough business to buy another limo, but lately those grannies, guess they ran out of them up north or something, because I don't see so much of them anymore."

"And you know this, Frank, because you're a businessman, but now I have to take any job I can get, I have to pay off that second car. It means I take business I wouldn't normally take."

Cliff, he must've got a look from Dad, because they both stopped talking and instead stared at the ground.

"Happy Birthday, Kid," Cliff said, he got down on his knees so he could reach down and shake my hand in the pool. He held his hand out with his palm open. He looked like he was rehearsing for a part he wasn't going to get. He had a look on his face, he wanted whatever was going to work out between us to work out.

"**CLIFF WILL BE TAKING YOU** out for your birthday," Dad said, he had his arms folded and he was looking down at the tile of the patio.

Dad and all the lies started that day. "I'm going to be a better father to you." Here's where it started. And me, with my pool and my sunshine, I didn't know what "a while" meant.

"I've heard so much about you, kid," Cliff said. He winked at me, like he'd known me all my life. Dad made a slight coughing sound that told Cliff to slow down a bit, that this would all be explained eventually.

Their shoes, Dad's penny loafers and Cliff's blown out leather uppers, I swear I could see some electrical tape when I looked hard enough, the same color as the rest of his shoes.

Birthday, Jesus, at a meatball parm, I'd forgotten my own birthday.

Bella Vista

CLIFF

SEEING CLIFF FOR THE first time was a stand-up comedy routine. What sort of person still believed that what separates humans from the animals was a cheesy suit and a poofy black hat?

Those eyebrows on him reached up and mingled with the creases on his forehead. Creases that came down to where his hand rested on the gold rim of his black limo driver's hat.

So there's Cliff looking like he's about to do me the biggest favor ever, and I had just lost my mother to a black hole of ego and drugs, and all Dad could do was sit there with a look on his face like he never told me on the way down here that he would be a better father.

There's a space for me to say something, but what do I say when my father was telling me he was turning me over to somebody else.

I'd like to think I was staring at Dad's face when he said what he said next, but I was taking in all that Cliff was.

"Cliff will be taking care of you for a while," Dad said.

Dad, we were in town for no more than fifteen minutes and already he was giving up. Turning me over to the first adult who walked through our gate. All that rage and what was I to know about it, it just felt as big as all of my big feelings did, and I did to that one what I always did to emotions I didn't know what to do with: I swallowed it.

I had to get a closer look of who my latest surrogate father was going to be, so I got out of the pool, and Dad was headed inside and I took that towel and dried off standing there in my wet underwear, and Cliff, poor bastard, he had to stand there. Dad wasn't looking at me, he was staring down at the black scuffs on his faded penny loafers. I covered up my underwear with my towel. The pattern my drippy towel made on the patio was one of those tests they give to people to see if they are crazy, because I was going crazy.

I still had to put on my shorts and my polo shirt. And then I was ready, to supposedly walk out of a house I just got to, in a city and state I just moved to, and start a new life on a new day with a new Dad I'd just met.

I was so new to Florida I was still adjusting to how the humidity was messing with my gravity, I wasn't ready for this. Cliff wasn't big on introductions, he said. "Beauty before age," and I went first.

My Dad had one of his leather boat shoes on the chair by the table. Sunglasses on, smile ear to ear. He'd made it; he didn't need me anymore.

I was leaving, and I'd only just arrived.

Dad, when he said: "This is Cliff, he'll be taking care of you for a while." He meant "I'm too busy to be your Dad." And that whole: "I'm going to be a better father to you shtick, let's just go ahead and pretend that didn't happen." And at the end, at some point, he'd say "Love you, pal," and that will be enough to make him feel decent enough about abandoning me.

Cliff, I knew Dad didn't like having to leave me with Cliff, even if I didn't *know*. Cliff told me in the way he held onto his body that day in the driveway. Cliff with his patches of orange light hitting Cliff's facial hair. His eyes were so round they bulged outside his eye sockets, all those things said, "Yeah, I know this is wrong, but what can you do?"

When Cliff put his hat on, when he wrapped his hairy, knuckled hands on the steering wheel, I saw a guy who pleased people for a living.

Cliff's limo was a 1980 white Cadillac Fleetwood, the kind of car a mobster with a love affair with leisure suits would drive. Inside, Cliff's limo smelled like warmed-up parmesan, marinara and cigars. The whole interior, from front to back was laid out in white leather.

There were two seats in the front, a bench in the back and this sliding window between them Cliff called the 'partition.'

"You ride in front," Cliff Said, "you always ride in front, the client sits in back. Get in, he said, pointing to the passenger side we're going somewhere," he let that pause last for as long as it took me to get in the car and sit down. "Fun."

The sign outside the joint said *Swenson's Old Tyme Ice Cream Parlor.* I didn't know it then, but the phrase "Old Tyme" was code.

What words like "Old Tyme" meant was white men wanting to go back to the way the world was before, according to them anyway, we all went nuts.

I was starting to figure out how there was this whole other level to language. Words meant way more than just describing the things they were supposed to describe. Words like *old tyme* were stand-ins for other words.

You could say "old tyme" and not be a racist. But if you said what you wanted to say, "Let's turn the clock back on civil rights."

Whoever invented the phrase "old tyme" wanted life back to when men were men, and women knew their place and ice cream parlors had people dressed in white shirts and ties, and black people weren't let in, if you wanted to say things like that, then you had to do it by putting the words "old tyme" in front of your store name. Forget about Cuban refugees and the world going to hell. You couldn't say that on a sign, but you could say Old Tyme and let people figure it out for themselves.

So we're there, at Swenson's, with a statue in the corner of Apollo only instead of pecs there are scoops of ice cream.

And this was the sweet part, Cliff knew exactly why I wasn't finishing the sundae.

Cliff's face, the soft around the edges of him. The way even a half-decision was up for negotiation.

"Your Dad told me about your Mom," he said.

I just met the guy and already he cared. Not only did he look right at me, but he put his hand on mine.

"They're called 'Swisher Sweets,'" he said, before he turned to light it. He did it so I wouldn't have to breathe in the smoke. "These little beauties are gonna kill me."

"Buddy, I've got no experience with anything like this," he said. The ice cream scoops had turned into this soupy tri-colored mess. "But no one deserves that."

HOURS LATER, I'M STILL SITTING at the marble counter bar with Cliff. He's gone through at least four Swisher Sweets.

My sundae was all soup. Layers of red and white and a little bit of brown curved up to a tall spoon sat in the dish, with a reflection of the ceiling fan above us. I took out the spoon, and saw the reflection of my face one year older.

Getting over losing my Mom and moving down to this strange place was going to take a hell of a lot more than three scoops of ice cream.

BUT HEY, AT LEAST I finally had someone who cared. I had Cliff and a racist old tyme ice cream parlor, trying to put me back together again.

I told Cliff about Dad and the Dirty Hippie, about how the Mom thing went slow, then fast. About DeadbirdRedbird. I told him about how I puke when I get upset. And then he put his hand on mine. His eyes couldn't meet mine, until they could, and he placed himself to where he could really see me.

You go through your life just wanting a friend, and then you find one and you realize what you've been missing.

But the night didn't end with the Swenson's Old Tyme Ice Cream Parlor, I had to experience the whole client situation.

The client, as in the people who pay money to have Cliff drive them around. The guy who sits on the other side of the partition.

Once Cliff laid down the *I care about you kid* shtick, then he had to lay down the ground rules. Of what I'm supposed to do and not do when a client is in the car.

I was beginning to realize just how long the phrase "a while" meant.

"Rule number one is all about the partition," Cliff said. He lit another swisher.

"It's the goddamned secret weapon kid; it's the thing people ask for.

"**This here partition is covered** in carpet, when it's up you cannot be seen, but if it's down and if you can see the client through the partition, then they can see you, and you cannot be seen, not once." It sounded fishy to me.

Rule number two. "When the partition is down, you crouch down, you pull up your legs, and you put your head between them. Any other position than that and they can see you. You do that as soon as you hear the sound of the partition working."

Rule number three. "You're gonna see some scary stuff, but know this, I'll keep you safe. That's a promise. We're going to have fun, but there'll be some stuff we gotta deal with. This is until you start school, so we're only talking about a few weeks, tops."

School, my god. I still had to tackle school.

School was Cliff dropping me off in front of the building. School was a yellow building, with lots of courtyards and the loudest bell I ever heard. School was fences and concrete and a student store that had the same pencil smell as the rest of the building. School was gray flooring, school was day after day after day. School was no one talking to me, school was fifth grade and memorizing phylums, school was waiting all day for Cliff to pick me up. School was the part I wanted to skip over to get to the fun part.

School was all the things that weren't worth learning. I knew more about life from the back of Cliff's limo than I ever did in school.

"This is what separates us from the client," he said.

And all of this was cool and all, but I was still thinking about what my Dad had said about Cliff taking care of me for a while, well that and about Cliff taking me out for my birthday. Until Dad said that, with all that happened, the changeover in parental duties, drastic change of location, with all of that, I didn't even know it was my birthday.

I can't believe there was ever a year when I forgot where my birthday was. Back then I had so much more on my mind than candles and cake.

Dad knew it was my birthday, and he didn't say anything until just then. This birthday thing was a thing to save for later, and later was Swenson's Old Tyme Ice Cream Parlor, this weird, Fifties throwback with a Roman marble finish thing to everything.

I was sitting in front of this ridiculous triple scoop ice cream sundae. One scoop was for Mom.

The second scoop was for Dad.

The third scoop was for Cliff, even if I didn't know him well enough yet.

This ice cream didn't taste like ice cream usually does. The sweet and the cream was there, but the enjoyment part of a birthday, but without Mom there on my tenth birthday, each bite was cold dread spread out from my throat to my chest.

Cliff was trying to tell me something. He saw me there, the look on my face. Ice cream on my birthday, I couldn't even enjoy ice cream on my birthday.

Cliff's coughing, and he put his hand on my shoulder, started to pull, I thought he had something to say to me, but when I turned my head to look over at him, his eyes were heavy like the clouds when they're ready to start raining.

"If my Dad cut me loose on my birthday I'd be pissed off, too," he said.

When Cliff said those words, it was the first time I ever heard somebody else acknowledge how fucked up my life was. He didn't tell me to suck it up. Cliff called it for what it was: A father abandoning his son.

There was this long, tan thing Cliff had between his fingers that looked like a cigarette but the smoke smelled sweeter than most cigarettes, like normal tobacco dipped in molasses. "They were big in the 70s, kid, so they smell to me like a cheap lawyer's office. Cheap leather chairs with the stuffing falling out" Cliff said, "or so they tell me anyway. One day those health nuts are going to take these beauties away from me. Swishers and Meatball subs, that's what I live on."

Bella Vista

FRAUD

O**NE OF THOSE FIRST** nights in the limo and already Cliff's pager was going off several times an hour. That first client, the one before the ice cream, was an airport pick up, a Nigerian father and son and their bodyguard.

The clothes they wore, matching suits and ties. Little pin on their cufflinks, the gold-plated flag of Nigeria. I didn't know where Nigeria was on a map, and judging from Cliff's response he didn't either.

"So where you from?" he said.

"We are from Nigeria. We are in town," the father said. His voice, the way it sounded, his words, the intersection of French and patois. "For meetings."

In a few minutes, I was about to find out that these two were royalty, like king and prince kind of royalty. That's who was back there.

Of course, I didn't know any of this at the time. I think Cliff did, but he didn't tell me. Besides, I was supposed to stay down in that little compartment where you put your feet in the passenger side seat.

The father was so composed. With the kid, though, you could tell he had no idea what was happening to him.

This kid sat there like he knew he was stuck more than just physically between his father and bodyguard. This kid had a bit of an afro, and skin so light it looked pale, which I'd never seen on a black person before. His face had this natural frown, like it had been on him since birth. The suit he was squashed into was dark gray and a tie the color of spilled red wine. From where I was, on my knees kneeling on the passenger seat, looking through the partition thing. I couldn't get my eyes off of him. That kid was me, only worse off. He had to publicly support his dad no matter what he did. They'd lied, they'd cheated. Only thing was, the boy didn't do any of it. This was all his father's doing.

I had to get down pretty fast. The Dad and bodyguards were starting to stare just to Cliff's right, which meant I had to dive back down.

But there was this moment, right before Cliff dropped them off, and a bodyguard got out on each side, and this kid's father stepped out, too. And the Dad was talking to Cliff about where to live, they were used to all this wealth and power, and now they had to find the cheapest possible place to stay.

They all got out, except for the kid. He was still sitting there, a look on his face like he was still back at the palace before the dream came crashing down.

I got back up and knelt on the passenger side seat. Screw the rules, this was a kid who was in such a similar situation to mine, a father who was doing something shady, who had to flee their home in the middle of the night, just like Dad and me.

I knew he'd seen me earlier. All he had to do was lift his eyes back up to where he got a straight look at me. He didn't smile, he didn't move, he had this sadness you could feel. There were no friends, or brothers or sisters, just him and his Dad that had done this thing that meant they had to leave.

But I didn't know anything about this. On that afternoon in the back of the limo. All I knew was this kid had a powerful Dad and he had to live in his shadow.

"Father says this is temporary," he said. He looked back down to his shoes, like the plan of what was supposed to happen next was written on them. "We'll be back in the palace, soon."

I didn't understand. In Miami there were all these connections to countries I'd never even heard of before, now they were running through my life like so many miles of jagged white lines going down the streets of Miami.

"I don't know why we are here," he said, "this is a vacation, this is what father said."

He only moved what he needed to move to get his words out. Only the essentials that were needed to speak were used: throat, lips, tongue, eyes.

"We lived in a palace. We had servants."

"What happened," I said.

The kid, still with his minimal face expressions. But this was the part where he couldn't look at me anymore. "It was the people, they couldn't take it, we had all the money and they had nothing." I saw in him a sadness so deep, it had scooped out the rest of who he was. "They fought back," he said. "They got their country back and now we're here."

And there it was, the falling away of my confusion, watching it go. Someone who lost all of who they were, but at the same time, it was like the universe was righting a wrong. It wasn't right that his family had all the money but the people were starving. And this kid, with all that he lost, he had to know that what had happened was a right correcting a wrong, but I can't know if he ever got to that place, because it was only a moment before his father put his hand on his shoulder, he couldn't bring the rest of his body into the limo. Just a hand on his shoulder, and in a way it was a good thing too, because I was breaking the rules.

After the kid followed his father. The kid's belt buckle he wasn't even buckled in. He slid over on the back bench seat, but before he did, he looked right at me. The boy didn't say a word, but in a way he did. His face told me, you have it so much better off than you even know.

And did I know then, what he would do, that years later he would be arrested for practicing law without a license? And how he claimed to be a sovereign citizen. And all of the stuff that was to come later on in the years, the constant jail time, the fraud, I think it all came from that one moment in the back of the limo. The look on his face, how he was already ruined. His Dad and what his Dad taught him. Status and the show it can be. How up front there's all that dazzles, but the back side, there's nothing to back it up. And there was something else, who I was, all the things that had happened to me, they still weren't anywhere as close to what this kid had to go through, compared to him, my life was a vacation. I didn't have Dad just then and at the time it didn't look like I'd be seeing Dad at all. I was hurt and confused, being on my own and still figuring out Cliff, but in a way, I was more free than I'd been in years.

Just before Cliff dropped me off, when I was beginning to feel something that could be called comfort, this weird song came on the radio.

The saxophone was the first thing to set him off.

"You gotta turn this one up, Kid," Cliff said.

Then the bassline, the singer's voice.

"I'm going to harden my heart."

"Something about the whole package that was," the saxophone, the singer's voice and that lonely bass line, the wet streets at the end of a night with Cliff, it was me and him while the rest of the city got into their own dark business.

Bella Vista

SUBS

THE WALLS INSIDE MIAMI Subs were covered in blue Hawaiian shirt patterns. There were ceiling fans going, and they gave off a light hum in the otherwise silent restaurant. We took one of the booths by the window, so Cliff could see the Fleetwood. We ordered two large meatball parm specials. Two cokes.

"All of my day's nutritional allowances can be fulfilled by eating one of these little jewels." Cliff said. "Unless I'm working."

He started telling me about how some nights he'd end up at a place where all the limo drivers get free catered meals. Cliff would take a client to one of these big steakhouses like La Fortuna. He'd pull up to the place, he'd park in back with the rest of the limo drivers. The owner would step out and see all the drivers and he would greet them in the parking lot.

Cliff leaned into me, his head was down below his shoulders.

"It's kind of a beautiful thing," he said. "The owner walked out and saw us sitting out there and forked out all of these little to-go boxes."

The kitchen staff had filled them with steaks, on the house, even brought out some mashed potatoes and onion rings.

"They'd bullshit and eat," Cliff said, "They'd sit behind the wheel, listen to all-night talk radio, and smoke cigarettes until their clients were done wining and dining."

"Not a bad way to spend an evening." Cliff said. "When it happens."

EVEN THOUGH IT WAS MY birthday and there was no cake, or even a mention of it, this guy had clearly forgotten about my whole day altogether, and yet, I didn't mind the forgotten birthday. Cliff told me story after story and smoked his Swisher Sweets, and my job was to listen.

Cliff ran Cliffs, his limo company. He'd taken off the black limo drivers cap. His Jheri-curled hair was molded to his head. He loosened his tie, unbuttoned his shirt, and I got a whiff of him, the sweat, smoke, and the new-carpet smell of the Jheri curl. He told me how he grew up in Brooklyn. He told me about how he and Dad were from the same neighborhood, how they went to the same high school.

Cliff stared out at Big Daddy's Nightclub across the four-lane road, at the limos that flooded the parking lot. From where we were, it looked like some of the drivers were eating out of little to go boxes.

"You want my life story" Cliff said, "here it is. "The story started with Cliff's Dad, a career electrician, "they used to say he lit up the streets of Manhattan with neon."

Well the years went on and Cliff got older and his Dad got older, and he retired from the neon sign business, and moved the contents of the family home in Park Slope down to a retirement community in Miami. Two months later, Cliff got married and the last of their possessions went down to Miami, to take care of his Dad.

"I figured", Cliff said, "there are all these old people coming down from Manhattan. They got a little money to burn, and they go from living in all of that luxury up there, to down here, where they were being carted around by a bunch of hospital orderlies."

"Let me tell you it was disgusting, these World War II guys weren't being driven around in stretch limos with full bars and frosted glass partitions, the cars they were driven around in were practically hearses."

Cliff figured he could treat these old guys right, pick them up in his Limo, charge a reasonable rate, and he'd be in.

So he bought the Fleetwood, started his limo business, and Cliff's Dad died, and over the next few years, one by one, his Dad's friends died too, and they weren't replaced by new waves from Brooklyn. "Instead," Cliff said, "Miami became this mix of crime and corruption."

Bella Vista

Our food came on two brown plastic trays. The meatball sub, and the way it was wrapped in wax paper, looked like a wound. The sub was a little taste of Brooklyn in parmesan and tomato sauce.

Cliff got a little sauce on his mustache, grabbed a wax napkin out of the dispenser between us.

"So there I am, in 1978 with a limo business and no customers," he said. "I'm driving down Miami Beach, I'm driving down Collins Avenue, and I'm driving down Ocean Drive in the middle of the night. There's no money coming in, and my pop is dead and gone."

"It was only a matter of time before the players found me."

CLIFF PULLED HIS GAZE AWAY from the sub, from the big paper cup of soda he sipped on, and looked right at me so I knew, this was for extra emphasis. His wide lips under his half-moon mustache with a little bit of sub sauce, little black irises, his olive complexion.

"These players tip well, but I have my rules, I won't have illegal activity in my limo."

"It's all about Bonnie." Cliff said. "I won't let her be wronged"

"Besides, I have my sweet Lucy to take care of me."

"Is that your wife?" I said.

"No," he said," it's my gun."

"But don't worry kid," he said, "I got it stored somewhere where you will never get to it, don't you worry about that."

This limo we drove around in, the way Cliff drove me around in it in all night, how his mood lifted when he opened up the door, when he started up the engine and rolled the partition down, how clean he kept it, I knew he was in love with her, from the headlights to the taillights, to the engine inside.

"Why Bonnie?" I said.

"Because she purrs like a Bonnie."

It was two in the morning, and my mind was ready for sleep. I sat in that front leather bucket seat on the way home, the slick of tires against Miami night rain, the talk radio station still talking about the longest football game that had just happened at the Orange Bowl, the Miami Dolphins versus the San Diego Chargers. Different sounds came together in my head. My refugee fell down by his tent under the freeway. "Te Quiero."

My body was in the Limo, but in my head, I'd never left Park Slope. It was one of those afternoons where Mom painted my portrait. I was on the floor, with the living room carpet warm on my neck. The house was dark and she sat at her normal spot in her studio, dipping that brush of hers into the paint cup. Mom's black transistor radio pumped out sports-talk about the big playoff game. "Cefalo's play was glorious," a caller with a heavy Brooklyn accent talked about how "If that touchdown had been called back, it'd be the Dolphins heading to the Superbowl."

In my head I was In the living room. Mom kept adding to her canvas with her long strokes of brush, and the light from her window, all of that Park Slope mid-afternoon shadow faded out, and what faded in was the mottled grass of a football field, and I no longer felt carpet on my neck but the warm grass in the big open field of the Orange Bowl, with white lines going down the field every ten yards. The game was over and Mom stood over on the other side of me, trying to get the light from the stadium high beams on my face just right. On the sidelines, the last Dolphins walked back to the locker room with their helmets off, the score still lit up on the scoreboard: 41 to 38.

Mom stood by her easel, still dipping that brush of hers into the paint can. Right there on the field open issues of Artforum were on the field, and the pages were turning from the almost nothing breeze inside the stadium.

Mom looked at me with all the love and the patience she had before she got into drugs. Mom leaned in to say something, but all I could hear was the sound of her radio, playing the sports-talk from the Fleetwood. "They'll be talking about this for years," one of the callers said, "the Epic in Miami, the one no one should have lost."

Mom looked over at me, reached out with a touch on my cheek. She turned away to wash a paintbrush, and just before she turned back around to face me, the stadium lights that shone down on me all went dark.

And what came to me then was the saxophone from Harden My Heart. The whole song started up in the middle of my dream.

I'm going to Harden My heart. I'm going to swallow my tears.

I'm going to turn and leave you.

Book One 1980 / Subs

Mom was gone. She didn't say goodbye. On the field around me, there was no table, no paint cans, no portrait for me to see. Just me and the fifty-yard line, the grass still warm from battle. All I had in this world was a view of the stands, the shadows of orange and aqua, the rows of empty seats drifting off into the blackness of night.

Bella Vista

SANCTUARY

A FEW DAYS LATER I was home from school. I was walking around upstairs. I felt like I was floating through these rooms. Next to mine was the fresh vacuumed carpet of what used to be an office. Smells of old wood, and synthetic nothing of the carpet cleaner. Next to the office was a bedroom, where my sibling would go if I had a sibling. The empty room had a ceiling fan, and there were clean vacuum lines on the carpet. The view was the same from my room, angles of sailboats, a canal going all the way to Biscayne Bay.

I was missing Mom, so I grabbed Mom's wedding ring from my desk. Held it close in my hand, so the diamond and the ridge it lived in dug into me.

I walked by the tall window going from top to bottom in front of the carpeted stairwell. Through the glass there was a view of the patio, the pool, and the hot tub just beyond it. The patio had a whitewashed coral finish to it. A wall around the front of the house protected us from the mangroves across the street.

The bubbling pool and patio furniture. A thermometer bobbed around, going underwater and rising back up again. I wanted to be that thermometer. I wanted to live half submerged.

Downstairs all that stood between me and the pool was the click of the front door and my feet warm on the coral of the patio.

I took off my shirt, and let it hang on the chair by the pool. I was down to my underwear when I dove in, the cool from the pool pushed the hot part of my brain into a small compartment inside my head.

I did the thing I did when I want to go deep. I kept my mouth closed and I blew air out of my nose. I did this until I laid my back down on the scratchy bottom of the pool. The view from down here, the bends and bubbles of light dancing on the surface was the world changing around me.

Down here with the weightless feeling of my organs neatly contained in my body, I saw something that I saw on that first day, something that looked like a window on the side of the deep end of the pool. My breath was almost running out. I pushed up and there was a burn in my lungs before I reached the surface. I opened my mouth. I breathed in every molecule.

I headed back down. My arms pushed the water around me closer to the deep end. My eyes stung a bit from the chlorine. I swam closer. There was a window, cut into the side of the pool, about halfway up the wall. Something to be seen on the other side of that window. The shrinking space of air in my chest. Open space and shadows, a room underneath the pool.

The house was still so new to me, I didn't know where I was going, but I had to get there. I dripped water through the kitchen and down a stairwell. I wandered through a few rooms. I saw what could be my in, a wall with a long cut down the front, a closet latched by a wooden handle.

I slid the wedding ring onto my fattest finger, and Mom, if you could have seen me put my weight behind that little door. If only you could have been there. The cracks of blue light opening bigger, me in a bath of blue light in the middle of all that dark. A gravel path, big stones to step on, and at the back of the room, was the window, thick head of chlorine smell, humidity.

Me and the window, and all that blue light that never stopped moving. Caribbean ocean-perfect. Like if you took every aquarium you ever saw, and added heavy doses of vacation brochures, even a whale nature program or two, you still wouldn't come close. There was something holy in there.

Next to the window was the pool pump with its handles and tubes.

Mom, if you could have seen me, with sore bits of gravel, down on my knees, bathed in that blue. Your eyes were seeing me as only you did, filling in all the dark places, plenty of light for you to paint me in.

There was so much blue in this little space that the room couldn't hold it all in. The light from that window was warm on my face, bubbles and yellow from the sun up there mixed in with that blue. Down here time stopped. Down here I was alive in a place just for me, a secret, a sanctuary.

There was a deep hum sound I could feel in my chest, a hum that was probably the pool pump turning on. There were clear PVC tubes just above my head and they started to shake. A hissing sound and the clear tubes got filled with water, yellow streaks and all that blue, sunshine and ocean.

As loud as the pool pump hum was, there was something soothing about it, a breath, a sound that filled up my ears and my throat. The pool pump hum bending me inside and out, the same rhythm as waves, a breath I could breathe with.

With the blue in front of me, the pool pump breathing for me, and tubes of liquid sunshine beamed above me, my breath was pumped through with chlorine and light.

Through this window I saw how much my life could change. That it's all in the wanting to. An hour ago my face looked like it was dipped in ash, but there I was breathing in sunshine and ocean and every second was full of the kind of being-a-little-kid-wonder I thought I lost when I moved down to Miami.

This room, my chapel, my secret. When the shit got too much I could come down here, with sunshine and ocean, with the pool pump breathing for me, I could live on Bella Vista with a hardly there Dad. I could live half submerged.

I laid down on the gravel. I stretched out in all that warmth. With the pool pump breathing for me, I closed my eyes and felt the back of my eyelids sweat. I got this movie-playing-in-another-room feeling. I held on as long as I could, but there was something in the heat and the bright, and even though I was right there on the gravel, I fell asleep.

The hum of the pool pump kicked on again. Opened my eyes and I saw their reflections bending in the window. They were walking around up there, stretched out in shadows of Dad and his ballooning abdomen, his spidery legs walked with someone close behind, the smooth edges of water melded into the shape of a black cocktail dress.

I brushed off a few bits of gravel, I tore out of there. I made sure to put the wooden latch back exactly where I found it. The pool pump hum gave me one last assisted breath on my way out. I closed the door on the last streaks of blue.

Bella Vista

STOWAWAY

ONE NIGHT WE PICKED up this woman who looked more like my mother than that woman I'll never know. Some nights I still think it *was* her.

She had red hair, of course. We picked her up in this dodgy part of town. North Miami. You could tell how rough it was by how few people were out. Lots of trash, padlocked doors, bars in windows, it took us a long time to get there.

WE PULLED UP TO A bus stop on a dark street. This woman, I was scrunched down into my little area, the partition thing down. I definitely wasn't looking at her but that color of red went across my peripheries like fire.

Cliff had told me before we got to this neighborhood, that this was one of those special fares, the kind he took just to keep his business afloat. This woman needed a ride. She needed some privacy. Extra important to stay hidden.

"It's not our job to judge, kid." Cliff said. "That's for the rest of the world to do."

CLIFF WAS GETTING A LARGE sum of money so she could do what she needed to do, And this woman liked the company Cliff gave. Thing was, she never paid a cent. Someone was paying this fare, but we never met them. All the times we picked her up, I still never knew who paid the tab.

It looked like she didn't know anyone well off. With her sky-blue denim shirt, matching jeans with a hole in the knee before holes in the knee became a thing. White flip flops and red hair and pale skin. Mom's skin was more reddish, like it was always in the middle of some blush.

This was Mom without any of her elegance. Her pale skin, the way her eyes wouldn't catch me when she spoke. She was in this car to do one thing and she liked looking at Cliff when she did it. It was all about when she plunged the needle into her vein.

She had to have someone she could look at when she fell asleep on the seat back there.

Cliff gave me a funny look when I first sat up, shook his head no, He hit the button, the partition and the robotic sounds it made going up and down. Cliff knew, no matter what was in my way, it was only a matter of time before I was back up there looking. I mean, how could I not?

"Keep that thing down" she said. "It helps me feel more okay."

"Kid," Cliff said, "this is Karla, Karla, this is the kid."

All the things I wasn't supposed to see was right there in front of me, her needle, and the belt around her arm. The look on her face when she slapped her veins with the rounded edges of the syringe in her mouth. I couldn't actually look when she stuck the needle in her arm. I mean, I knew what she was doing. I still couldn't look down at her arm. I had to look at her face instead, at the relief, like she was sick and only now she was better. With this ritual of hers, a spoon, a cotton ball, a drop of clear liquid.

And Cliff, was he bothered by this, was he freaked out? Not once did he even make a face. He knew what she was doing and he kept on driving like this was all normal. Like it was all there in the contracts they signed each night. Cliff did what he was paid to do, to keep on looking forward.

Sometimes I think maybe I just wasn't looking hard enough, because it doesn't really matter if it was her or not, in a way it was Mom.

Maybe it was her and I just didn't want to believe it was her. That she had followed me down here like some smacked-up ghost. I mean a woman with red hair wanted to shoot heroin in the back of the limo Cliff and I practically lived in. And yeah I know that Cliff didn't know what color hair my Mom had. But he knew about Mom's drug problems. If this picking up a client and the whole point was for her to have company while she shot up, and someone was willing to pay good money for this, if all of this didn't sound believable, then you don't know Miami and the characters that came in and out of that limo.

This lady wanted the partition down so she wouldn't be alone, so she could see faces and hear voices and do all the normal things people have to do when they are stuck together on long car rides. Those in between conversations, they can be the stuff of life.

I had to watch her. Really take it all in. And from that point on the mystery of mom wasn't a mystery to me anymore.

She wanted to shoot up with people in the car, because I suppose it made shooting up look like what she was doing wasn't totally fucked.

"I need someone right here with me," She said. "Just in case something happens."

LIKE AN AIR BUBBLE TRAVELING from the syringe to her veins, or if she overdosed. She had Cliff to drive her straight to the emergency room. She did this so she didn't end up in the back of some strange cab or an abandoned vehicle.

"We still cool on the deal, Daddy-O?" she asked.

Then she got up, leaned forward and put her cheek next to Cliff's. She didn't see me, she didn't even look down in my direction.

"What does mama like?" Karla said. Same time as Cliff. They said it together. The two of them had it down.

"Mama likes the good stuff," Cliff said.

And then it came out from the glove compartment, all those badass R&B singers, Luther Vandross, Teddy Pendegrass. He slipped in the Luther, those songs were bumping and they both knew every word.

So Cliff knew I knew and was fine with all this, this woman shooting up in the back of Bonnie. And to see this thing happening, the whole ritual of it. The time she took, waiting for just the right second. Just like she did before, on all those other nights. How all of it when she did it, this was the sick that was going to make her better.

After a while. I sat up in the seat, like a normal person would sit. Sat in the chair and looked out at the buildings sliding by. The night taking over the Miami skyline. Water, trees and the R&B. The next time I looked back there, she was asleep.

"Sometimes you're gonna see stuff you shouldn't." Cliff said. "It's not always pretty, but she needs someone, and it might as well be me. It's not easy to see, but it's who she is."

Cliff and what he taught me, that no matter how messed up we are, at some point we need to see and love people for who they are, mistakes and all.

When we dropped her off, we stopped right in front of this old motor hotel. It wasn't much. Two stories, this huge neon sign bent with the half oval shape of a Cadillac.

She was back there, still asleep. Funny how even drug addicts look peaceful when they're asleep. Here I could really look. Knees on the seat, my hands around the headrest. The kind of pants she wore corduroy dark green with the fringy orange top, casual but yet almost not quite falling apart. Her hair half in her face. That red hair, pale skin, big forehead. Long slim nose that came to a point. It was the kind of feature you could fall in love with, I didn't realize it at the time, of course. Her eyes opened and her body moved – a person moving from one plane of existence to the next.

"Hey you," she said. When she smiled there were parts of her cheek that turned red, just like Mom's.

"You're a stowaway," she said.

SHE HELD HER HAND OUT for me to take it. I went around to the Limo's back door by the motel, opened it for her, took her hand. And she wrapped her arms around me, like she knew I needed it because there are hugs when they come you realize just how much you need them. This woman, my Mom and not my Mom, this was me, on this trip and for all the rides we took her on, this was it. Me and Mom, for real this time, saying goodbye.

And I wonder what Cliff would've made of Mom if he was there in Park Slope when she was on her knees that night? Would he have left like Dad did, or would he have talked to her, let her know that he was there to help, not judge. Me, I was learning how to be a man in the front seat of a limo, from a driver and a drug addict.

Dad had no idea where I was.

KIKI

CLIFF AND THE PEOPLE we were picking up, there were nights where I was so afraid that someone was going to die in the back. Afraid that the cops would pull us over and someone like Karla would be scrunched over with a needle hanging out of her arm and Cliff would go to jail and Dad would find someone else to take care of me.

To Dad, taking care of me, meant picking me up and dropping me off, as for the hours in between, I was on my own.

I watched lot of TV.

The way it was going, each client we picked up was more fucked up than the last.

PEOPLE STUCK IN BAD SITUATIONS, people without any control over their lives. And then I met Kiki.

When those legs of hers came across the back of the limo I knew I was in trouble. The pink of her high heels, her leggings an even brighter pink than the shoes, blue wrap of a mini skirt, white blouse, sunglasses on, and the long luxurious locks of her long brown hair,

"Kiki, this is the kid," Cliff said. "Kid, meet Kiki."

KIKI, HER SMELL, THE WAY she spoke, the edges of her voice just went through my ears, into my lungs, and made a warm place in my chest where my breath lived. Breathed warm all over me, even to the places I wasn't supposed to talk about.

These places and what it was.

I DIDN'T KNOW SEX WAS A thing until I met Kiki.

It wasn't just how she talked, it was how she moved her body, too. Cliff had told me all about Kiki before we even picked her up.

"Kiki was one of my first real clients," Cliff said. "Once I lowered my standards, I couldn't go back." That right there was the start of Cliff's business model, which means you help the people that nobody else wants to help." Which meant Kiki was the gateway client between old ladies and people who did strange things for money.

Me right then and there in one moment figuring out that there were people that would not only pay for sex, but also that there were people whose primary job was to provide sex to those willing to pay for it. That sex was something that people wanted bad enough to pay for it. And I figured this out all at the same time.

Her body. That's what she sold.

HER JOB, THAT VOICE OF hers made the words that came out of my mouth all shaky. "What do you do, for work?"

"I'm a prostitute, honey," Kiki said. "I sell my body, for sex."

KIKI. FOR SOME REASON IT never really freaked me out. She was so nonchalant about it, like it was her own thing and no one else had to deal with it. She became one of our regular pick-ups.

Yes, she was someone who had sex for money, a woman of the night, a prostitute.

Really, at the end of the day, was it really such a big deal? People wanted her, and they had to pay, it was on her terms.

Kiki there, in back, Cliff didn't even try to cover her up. The partition never was up in the first place, I think after Kara, Cliff just didn't care. Why try to hold back the deep dark world when we were surrounded by it?

Kiki, that pink piping, white and pink lines going up and down, back there, one leg over the other, moving one leg, her sandals, bright pink nail polish.

She laid it all out. "When you are a prostitute," she said, she was snapping her gum between words between sentences. "Customers to me aren't called customers, they're called Johns."

Johns, all of her customers, and I mean all of them were called John. "Why John?" I said.

"No honey," she laughed, took those sunglasses off, so I could see those eyes, my god, they were blue, slushy blue eyes and jet black hair, I felt her even more present in the back of the limo, her and her sex had me pushed all the way back to the window. I couldn't think straight, I could hardly breathe.

"No honey, not one John, all of them are Johns."

"But why John?" I said, "Why not Paul, or George, or Ringo."

KIKI RIGHT THERE, JUST LOST all the seriousness on her face. A laugh that sent waves of warmth through me.

Those eyes of hers, came over to my side of the limo slowly, she used her eyes the way she used every other body part.

"I don't know if it's just that most of my clients are men," she said," but occasionally I get a woman."

Men and women and women and women, you step inside a limo, you miss one day of this class that life taught in the back of a limo and you miss the whole world going sideways.

She told me about her code of ethics. She didn't take Johns in the car. The John had to pay for the hotel room they'd use. The

John had to be the one who offered sex or the whole thing of the two of them wouldn't be a thing.

And it had to be at a hotel, a proper hotel, not a motel.

"THIS BODY MAY ROAR LIKE a motor," she said. Her eyes were swallowed up by her sunglasses, big round specs, you'd call it bug-eyed if the glasses didn't look so good on her. "But you Johns are going to have to take your time with me, you are going to pay for every single second."

Her legs had this white fabric to them, with pink piping all up to her legs, then the mini skirt. Angles that led to me seeing lines. I had thoughts that I didn't know what to do with. I was twelve, old enough to feel it, but too young to know what else to do. For me, sex was a feeling, not an act, well I imagined it had something to do with my penis, but that's about it.

I was twelve. I could still appreciate it, even if I didn't understand it.

HER FACE BACK THERE, THE moment where it was her in her sunglasses just staring out into space. Then I guess she figured I was staring at her.

"But not you though, honey," she said. "You are too young." I was always getting close to the good stuff when it ended.

Cliff so casual, like people who have sex for a living and people who need a safe place to shoot up, how both of these people were shunned by the rest of the world, but not in this limo.

I was a boy learning about the world though the people who society discarded.

Kiki, WHEN SHE LEANED FORWARD, the edges of her bazooms close to me, she smelled like cotton candy.

"Look, I know who I am," she said to me. "I have my rules."

Cliff let out a cough, we were driving down US 1, in Homestead, deep South Florida, Marshland.

"You weren't like that when we first met. Remember that." Cliff looked back at her for a second.

"You're always bringing up the old days."

Kiki rested her arm on my shoulder, that pink piping all the way down to her hands, She sat there looking at her nails. She'd already heard Cliff tell this story at least a dozen times.

Cliff lit up a swisher and let it sit smoking in the ashtray until it burned out, or I stopped breathing, whichever came first.

"I'm going to pick the two of you up," he said. "And already, this guy, he's onto something fierce. They were already arguing when I picked them up. I'm not driving for five minutes before I hear that sound that tells me he's hitting her. I knew what was going on, I didn't roll the partition thing down. Even though we were pulled over on the Rickenbacker Causeway, even though I pulled over to where there really wasn't room to walk with cars whizzing by. I went straight to the gun in the glove compartment. I told him, right then and there, to get out. Left him right there on the causeway."

Kiki, she was chewing gum, blew up a big bubble and let it pop. Cotton candy breath over my shoulder.

"Took me weeks to get work again," Kiki said, "but that john never came back."

Cliff, his eyes on me, a peek over his sunglasses, not in a friendly way, just long enough so no one else could see.

A gun, he had a gun in the glove compartment.

"**L**OOK, I WAS GONNA TELL you about exactly where the gun was." Cliff said, we were at Miami Subs, ceiling fans, meatball parms and smoke. "There never was a good time."

"It's only for our protection" he said. He had a mouthful of food, bits of tomato sauce showed when he spoke, the last bits of a swisher burning in the ashtray.

"I take your safety seriously, Jay," Cliff said.

DAD, I WISH HE'D DONE the same. I mean there I was, and I

loved Cliff, but each night I was out with people with questionable morals, cheats on the run, corrupt government officials, sex workers, drug addicts, I would listen to Cliff, I wouldn't judge, but Jesus Christ, isn't that why Dad moved me down to Miami for, to get away from all that Mom was doing. I had words to say to my Dad, and I was almost 13, I could handle him, now, on my own.

HOMECOMING

CAME HOME LATE ONE night. Got home and didn't have a key.

I wanted to believe that I willed the rods and pins and door sensors to open up on my command, but Dad just left the door unlocked.

When I first got into the house I wasn't sure if I had it in me, but when I made it upstairs and heard Dad's voice through his office door, I knew what I was going to do.

I was going to tell him he was a hypocrite, and with all of his high and mighty bullshit, that he was just as much of a bad parent as Mom.

There was an extended brass handle on the door between me and all the things I wanted to say. The door handle.

Closed my eyes and held my hand out to the handle and kept my mind cleared the way the telekinesis works in comic books. I turned the door handle, the big brass thing, and it opened up the way I'd willed it to, dragged against that carpet like it was dragged through mangroves. There was Dad's desk, the backs of Dad's picture frames, Dad's view of the canal, but no Dad. His voice came out of this black box on his desk, spat out in a sea of static of him and his greeting.

"You've reached Frank Pershall," his voice came out of the machine, "please leave a message."

The only thing that meant anything to me in Dad's office was written on one line of computer paper that smelled like burnt milk. The line said Cliff's limos and next to it was this long account number, some kind of connection to Dad. There were pictures of me and Mom on his desk, Park Slope, '78, back when Mom was still normal.

Went to my room. Locked the door. Threw my comforter down over my shoulders.

Turned my head to the wall, and counted the bumps in the stucco.

That sound, that fist of his and how hard it hit the door, it was like a code that sound.

Two and a half rounds of knocks banging on my door, in a way I kind of missed it. "Why is the goddamned office door open?" Dad said.

Dad, I don't know how he got in, but there he was right in front of my bed in his butterscotch tie and sky-blue shirt.

I didn't apologize or go all yessir no sir, I let him have it.

"**You left me**," **I screamed** so loud my throat burned. "You say you're going to be a better person then you leave me with some limo driver to be my Dad?" I loved Cliff more than my own father, but I didn't want Dad to know. "Where the fuck have you been?"

And after I took my stand, after I screamed at him the loudest I'd ever screamed, I was expecting that line of nerve that went from Dad's eyeball down to his neck when he gets mad to light up, but he said nothing.

He sat down next to me on that waterbed, with the waves of the bed sloshing all around. So close to this big man and what was I going to do, his thick arms and his chest and body, and he put his hands on my shoulder like ten billion parents have done since the beginning of time. His face just like mine with that perma-frown, the same one I had then, and the same one I have now.

The waterbed took a few seconds to stop moving. He had his hand on my shoulder, and this look on his face like he had so much to say to me he didn't know where to start. The view of the houses and boats and hard concrete.

Dad, with the twin rings of Gemini on his wedding ring, tried to push back on my shoulder. At first like when I was younger and he could just move me around. That grip of his was tight and fast and strong. He tried to push me back, so I'd be lying down on my bed.

But I didn't let him.

DAD TOOK HIS OTHER HAND and put it there on my other shoulder. Father and son and hands and shoulders sitting on the bed. He tried to push me back, and it took all the strength in my spine to fight back, to push back against him.

Dad, with all that leverage he had, I couldn't fight anymore.

I KEPT EXPECTING HIM TO SAY something, but he was using this silent thing that really freaked me out. I mean here he was reacting to what I said, but I had pissed him off so much he was out of words. I actually wanted him to say something to me then, that's how bad I wanted him to know.

What he'd done.

DAD WAS GETTING HIS WAY with me the way he always got his way, by being bigger and stronger than anyone else in the room. By pushing so hard down on my shoulders that they came down on my bed and I was on my back, with the waves of the waterbed underneath us. Dad and the weight of him there on top of me, the weight of his chest, arms. I'd been close to my father before, but not like this. His face, his sideburns and his pores of his thick boxer nose. There was his breath, so calm. His breath still had that old ginger cardboard smell.

I flipped over. I grabbed hold of the foam padding on the corner of the bed. He was still on top of me, and the only way he'd get off is if I forced him off.

Dad tried to grab the neck of my shirt, gave it a pull, a tug. Just a hint of what was gonna be next.

The bed was heaving from our bodies going at each other like we did.

I pulled a leg back, I fired off a kick with and I'm still not sure what part of him I hit, but it was hard and bony.

I pulled my leg back up, fired off another kick. There was no pull on my back. I jumped off that bed. I tore ass downstairs. I didn't look back.

I didn't stop to listen to the sounds of the footsteps. I was already there in my head.

My CHAPEL, MY SECRET, THE one place he couldn't find me.

Bella Vista

DEADBIRD REVISITED

I OPENED MY EYES, TOOK a breath and already there was something wrong with me. Felt like thick honey in my chest, each breath heavier than the one before. I couldn't get up, couldn't move, the heavy in my chest was the heavy in my legs too. I was lying there in my bed, the comforter over me. The X-Men issue by my bed, the one with Cyclops and Jean Grey in his arms on the cover, the pink light and the thick ink lines in the muscles of him holding her. And all of these things were things that would have put a smile on my face a few weeks ago, but right then I saw the man and woman in tights as the super hero kid stuff it was.

There was no point in pretending, I was alone and there was nothing a comic book could do about it.

My room, my wall of bookshelves, desk and mirror, waterbed next to the window overlooking the canal to Biscayne Bay. Slats from the ac vent making the slats of blinds clink together.

Big picture window in front of me, the lines and angles of the boats going all the way down to Biscayne Bay. It was a beautiful day, but all I saw was the darker edges of the shadows of the water, the big black, brown sludge color of the canal. A boat right in the back of our house, two big white engines on the back of a boat leaned up out of the water.

The feeling in my chest wouldn't let me leave. Dad and the bed and what I'd done.

I leaned over to my clock radio next to my bed, slid my forefinger on the black dial, changing stations, looking for my favorite song. The song was always on, it was just a matter of time turning the dials, the in between of static, the start of the thump of bass line, a saxophone ringing out of the darkness.

HARDEN MY HEART, **BY QUARTERFLASH.** Don't laugh. That song felt like the heavy chest that was living in me.

"I'm going to harden my heart," the lady sang, "I'm going to swallow my tears," and she said the next three lines with such a pause. She was going to enjoy every step.

"I'm going to turn and leave you."

Cliff wasn't going to pick me up for several hours, so I pulled my comforter back over my head, lost myself into the click of the ceiling fan, and when I opened my eyes again instead of being just a few minutes later. It was hours.

𝕴**T WAS DARK OUTSIDE WHEN** I woke up. It'd been hours since I'd eaten, but I still wasn't hungry. The heavy feeling in my chest saw to that, I couldn't stand, I couldn't get out of bed.

But Cliff was coming to get me, so I put on my pants.

𝕮**HE OPEN OFFICE DOOR NEXT** to mine was empty. Downstairs Dad's bedroom door was open too, his bed made, all the lights in the house turned off, the only light from the thermostat. Me, in the middle of the house, my feet cold on the tile, I was standing there, alone.

Got to the front door, and there's the salt smell from the mangroves, and the humidity, which made breathing even harder. Opened up that gate, down the steps to the driveway. Don't know how long I waited for Cliff.

I had to get out of that house. Stood in front of the driveway, stared out at the mangroves, and every once in a while a little bit of wind would come and bend the leaves one way. A car would drive by and I would think for a second it was Dad, then it hit me.

I didn't even know what kind of car Dad drove.

𝕮**LIFF, I COULDN'T WAIT TO** see him, couldn't wait to tell him what happened. That limo may have contained the whole fucked-uppedness of the adult world, but it was mine.

Finally the edge of the car turned down at the end of Bella Vista, and just like that, Bonnie pulled into our driveway all polished up and spit-shined. Two honks of the horn from Cliff. I went around to the other side.

My hand was on the door handle, my door right before I opened it. That tinted window with Cliff on the other side, the thing in my chest, the something I was coming down with was the window's reflection of who I was, a pale, sick kid in the middle of sunny Florida.

Went over and pulled that door open and slid into the front seat. Cliff didn't say anything when he looked over at me, because there was this rhythm of the things that we did and the order we did them in. I rolled my window down. I threaded the seat belt. Clicked it latch-locked, my hand had a little shiver to it when I shut my door, just a reminder that the thing that was in me was still there.

Cliff started the engine up. No music when we pulled out of the driveway. First time ever there was no music pulling out of the driveway.

"You look sick, kid." Cliff said.

How to open up your mouth and talk when you can't even tell what's wrong with you. Drove for a few blocks like this. More than a few blocks, all the way down the leafy overhangs of Old Cutler, then to the bustling traffic of Lejune Road then the buildings got taller and more spread apart, tall condos arcing up as far as my eyes could see out the limo. and at the corner of somewhere and Brickell I opened my mouth and the words just fell out.

"I kicked him."

CLIFF'S EYEBROWS UP, BOTH OF them. "Kicked who?" he said.

I was so angry at Cliff then, impatient, just wanting him to understand what I was going through.. Who? Who the fuck did he think?

"Your Pop?"

Yes, my fucking pop, Jesus Christ, my world turned and it took Cliff five goddamned minutes to notice.

And I thought Cliff would hear that and side with me, or at least listen to what I said, he was always such a good listener, but this time, he let me down.

"Jeez kid, but look, your Pop's paying me to drive you around, "he said. "So let's talk about the Dolphins or something."

Cliff, I had to admire him even if I hated that he couldn't talk about this, at least he was honest, and what came out of his mouth was how he felt, no bullshit.

Even with all of Cliff's can't-talk-about-Dad, I still felt relieved to talk to him, because, there was something about the act of opening my mouth and telling the one person I had to tell things to. And all of this was a small little bit of good squeezed between my chest and my stomach.

Don't know why I did it. I never stole a thing in my life, but there was the pack on the dashboard in front of me, open for the taking. Cliff's Swisher Sweets.

We were stopped at a gas station. Cliff moved a blue soapy sponge on a black handle around the driver's side window. I saw my chance, reached up for that pack, slid the top the rest of the way back, put a hard plastic Swisher filter between my thumb and forefinger. I didn't feel any sort of devil on my shoulder. Just slid two swishers out of the pack, even put the pack back exactly the way I found it, with the top of the pack leaned back on the dash in front of me.

Me, thirteen years old and already stealing from Cliff, and I didn't feel a thing. Nothing, nada. Zip.

I didn't just take two swishers, I took a lighter as well. He had so many, and how else was I going to smoke it. I took the smallest, pinkest lighter I could find, there were a whole bunch in the space for coffee mugs between our two seats.

I didn't feel anything but that sick, far away feeling, didn't even flinch when Cliff opened his door. Just put that palm of mine over the Swishers and the lighter.

I did all of this with Cliff right there, he didn't question me, not once.

LATER ON, AT THE END of the night. We pulled up into my driveway, the humidity when I stepped out of the Limo.

"Hang in there, kid," Cliff said. "Things always look better in the morning."

Cliff had no idea what I was going through, and he never did. Something in me wanted to grab one of the strands of Cliff's Jheri curl that were always hanging out of his cap. Wanted Cliff to feel what I felt.

As soon as Cliff pulled out of our driveway I had the pink lighter out and was lighting up my first Swisher. It did smell like a cheap lawyer's office, reminding me of the smell of basements back in Park Slope. My thumb on the wheel of the Pink lighter, the sweet on my lips from the sugary tip of the Swisher. A few flicks and my thumb was sore before the light up fire – cough – before the burn in my chest. The pain there, the burn. Kept going, even through all the coughing, hurting with every breath. As much as it hurt, as much as I coughed, the hurt was the only thing that felt good.

I WOKE UP THE NEXT DAY to the pictures in my head of black lung from the films they used to show us in health class and the burn in my throat was still there from the swisher I smoked. The click of the ceiling fan chain, the humidity, even inside there was humidity. The little green star stickers on the ceiling of my room from the last people who lived in the house. They were peeling away. And now this thing was living in me, in my chest when I breathed and in every drop of sunshine that came through my window.

I wasn't going to count on anything getting better. I closed my eyes and laid back down, got back under the comforter, and laid there, just listening to the sounds of the empty house, the squeak of the stairwell and what it meant, meant someone was on the stairs.

Me here in this place, under the blanket, the footsteps, the squeak of the stairwell. Dad and the way he puts one foot heavy down in front of the other. Dad, the person I've been ignoring, the guy who just two days ago I'd kicked was now on the other side of the door.

I closed my eyes, turned my body so I was facing the window, orange in my eyes and those floaty bug looking things I see when I'm tired.

The door sliding on carpet sound, Dad entering my room, as in breaking and entering because this sick I feel inside was from him.

And he wasn't content to just stand by the door, no, he had to walk over, sat down on the bed and put his hand on my side like he did when I was little and he'd come in to check on me, and I'd pretend to be asleep even when I wasn't.

"Jay," he said.

My name was on the tip of his tongue, the last time he said that was when we were driving down to Florida, and it felt like the whole world had changed since then.

I rolled over and opened my eyes and there he was right there. Yellow polo shirt, khaki shorts, and boat shoes.

Something in Dad's voice, not the usual angry snap. "I thought we could talk."

There was nothing really there for me to hate about him. He didn't have that fight in him, not just then. His eyes were red-blooded, but something else, not mad or angry or wanting to pull me down, those eyes of his had tears in them, never seen that before. Dad was always so strong, and there he was standing in front of me wanting to talk, maybe even willing to admit he was wrong.

And there was a part of me that wanted to talk to him, the little kid in me that still thought he could turn things around and this could be the beginning, but this thing in me had its own plans, and it took the things I wanted to say and made me turn back over to face the window, to the edges of black in every angle, in every sailboat, and every ripple of water heading out towards Biscayne Bay.

"Go find someone else to control," I said.

DAD THERE ON MY BED, his hand on my side, I was turned to the wall, not going anywhere, not budging one bit. My eyes tried to close out the orange world.

"I know you're angry," Dad said, "You've got every reason to be angry."

ALL THE THINGS I'D DONE and all the things he'd done and all the times I'd wanted him to say exactly this.

"I ignored you," he said. "I let someone else raise you."

I WANTED TO TURN AROUND AND see his face when he was apologizing and see what it looked like, as much as the little kid in me wanted to turn around and take him up on his sorry. Instead what I did was to keep staring out at the canal leading to Biscayne Bay, the black murk of the water. Heard that song in my head. *Harden my Heart.* A cold bead of sweat ran down my neck, the words in my brain before they came out of my mouth. Even with the pause, I knew that's just what I wanted to say. So I turned around and saw him there, those eyes of his opened up and tears down his cheeks, his boxer nose, his thick, veined hand on my side.

"It's too late." I said, "You can't just decide to be a better person."

DAD'S FACE THEN, THE STERN forward push to everything, never resting even for a second, and now all that was broken, his mouth up and down and white spaces showing up on either side of his nose.

"Can't you see that I'm here," Dad said, "that I'm trying?"

EVEN IN THAT MOMENT OF me on the bed and him there, as much as I wanted to have him in my arms again, all I could do was let the thing inside me talking for me.

I said, "I'm gonna take my backpack and walk out of here."

"**Y**OU HAVE TO KNOW THAT I had your best interests at heart," Dad said, "it's all I've ever wanted."

I got up, started pulling stuff from my drawers, and threw them into my backpack. Turned around in my doorway, carpet underneath my feet.

And I left. This wasn't the kind of leaving that you do when you're six and you walk to the end of the block and you come back five minutes later. This was the real kind.

RENEGADE

WALKED DOWNSTAIRS WITH THAT backpack. Walked the six blocks up Bella Vista Ave to the main road, by the construction site. Took the second Swisher I had stashed in my pocket.

Walked down the street with the trees down that grass strip of Bella Vista, fresh cut grass bumped up against the burnt rust smell of the mangroves churning up from across the street, the feeling that I'd gone all the way, I'd left him before he could leave me again.

Five blocks up, San Mateo, Nevada, Lerida, Deva, that little spit between Agua Avenue and the main road by the guard house, the street with all the construction sites.

The part of Bella Vista stopped at a construction site. I put my backpack down, sat on a pile of two-by-fours, lit up a swisher, I could see the whole of Bella Vista in front of me, where it started and where it ended.

The construction site was for a two-story A frame. The house was almost done, except for doors and windows. Walking through that house, I found a place to sleep in the bottom corner of the house. There was some old plastic wrap from the sheet rock I guess, some piece of plastic large enough I could use it as a comforter. I made a bed out of dead leaves and that big ass sheet of plastic wrap. And, yeah, it wasn't a full house, but it was more of a home than Bella Vista because it was mine. The A frame house was unfinished, like I was. I had a bed, I had a corner, I had a view of Bella Vista and every car that came up or down it.

That first day Dad and I got there, coming down Old Cutler, through the guard house, then the whole of Bella Vista spread out before me. I wasn't in control, Dad could've dragged me to Siberia and I wouldn't have boo to say about it, but now I was the one who was calling the shots. Me not feeling anything for walking out on Dad when he was so ready to apologize, maybe for the whole of it, taking me down here, the false promises, dumping me off on a guy who drives a limo for a living.

Sat there on that pile of two-by-fours, the little chill to the air, the sky getting darker, lights coming on from the houses down all the canals, last bit of reflection off the sun in the water. Then lights and fading daylight, the dark of light before it got dark for real.

I was tracking every car that drove by, not many not here in this subdivision, not on a late Sunday afternoon, looking out for Cliff, looking for Bonnie.

My eyes on the front ends of cars and lights and trying to build a picture of the car that is supposed to go on the other side of those lights, lights and after a while they all looked the same, and it was getting cold. I put my head down on a bag of cement and wrapped plastic around myself, and tried to fall asleep.

Tried to pick out the moment I knew would come, when Cliff would come to pick me up, he'd heard from Dad and would try and find me, that it would only be a matter of time before I heard Cliff's feet on that gravel on the construction site. I was trying to fall asleep on a pile of dead leaves. But there was nothing to keep out the world out there from the world in me.

Because it was right there, I was in this house, this unfinished home that was my home and the one guy I had left to save me didn't give a shit about me enough to find me, and I was only a few blocks from my real house. I was just a kid waiting for someone to come and save him. But nobody did.

Sleep when it came over, slivers of memory, sound of Mom's voice on a Sunday morning, painting me, and what that felt like, waking up to early morning and the smell of Mom's tea, that was actually the stink of the mangroves, humidity.

And I must've drifted off in the quiet between when I woke up the first time and when I woke up the second time. The second time, when you wake up and you know that there is another person standing there, the air feels that much more cramped, there is another person sharing the air that you breathe.

And the smell, too. I was half asleep but already I could smell the sweet of the swisher smoke that was on me too, but closer, more intense, a bite of a parmesan smell, marinara sauce right up in my face, then a hand. Opened my eyes and there he was, his mustache, the stupid limo drivers get up, the tie all loose around his neck, the white shirt that was a tea shade of brown from all the sweat and all the late nights and the smoke.

Cliff had something in his hands, he was carrying, when I stood up, he put it around me, it was a sport coat. Cliff must've had extras lying around.

He opened the door for me, he took his time, put his hand on my back and led me into Bonnie, and the familiar, stinky smell of home.

We drove back to Old Cutler, back to the highway, back to Miami Beach. "Looks like you could use a meatball sub," Cliff said.

SCHOOL

SO THE TIME COMES when they can't put it off any longer. Whatever delay existed between New York and Florida had expired. It was time for me to start school.

Dad didn't take me. It was Cliff, still tired from the night before. Me especially. I'd woken up on a pile of wood and slept off and on in the limo. Cliff was up the whole night with clients. Each time I woke up there was a different client. The music changed each time too, from the up and down piano riffs of salsa meringue, to the smooth R&B Cliff was all about, to the late-night early morning sounds of Classical or as Cliff said, "A little bit of culture goes a long way, kid."

WHEN I WOKE UP AGAIN we were in the half-moon driveway in front of my new school, Pinecrest Elementary. Squares in the concrete let too much light into the front of the limo. It was morning and already I had beads of sweat under my arms and legs. "Cliff", I said. I was still trying to remember what school was. "What about my lunch?" Cliff looked at me, I'll never forget it, like I had never been to school, it had been that long. "Kid, they have a lunch room," he said, "with a menu and everything."

Cliff handed me a packet with the words *sixth grade* written across the top in green permanent marker. *Mrs. Carter* was written in the penmanship of someone who drove prostitutes and junkies around but made sure to have this packet ready for me on my first day of school.

What Cliff did on that first day wasn't much but it was still better than what Dad would've done if he tried to take care of the whole school thing. At least Cliff got out of the car and walked me to where my class was.

Even introduced me to Mrs. Carter. She had shoulder-length black hair, I could tell just from her face that she was nice, if a little tired.

Mrs. Carter introduced me to the class and I sat down in one of those seat/desk combination chairs with a big swoop of chrome that held the two together.

"Class, we have a new student," Mrs. Carter said. I did a quick look around, a girl with a gray-haired afro had these blue eyes that didn't look at me, they looked through me.

"This is Jay Pershall," She said to the class. She leaned her hand on mine, fingertips on my shoulder. I think I might've blushed. "He's from New York."

Mrs. Carter told us about how we were going to learn to take notes, said it would make us better students, so we could get into college and get jobs like our parents had.

She told us to write *on* the dividers I got in the packet with the rest of the stuff Cliff gave me, manila-colored thick sheets with colored tabs on them. Notebook paper inside each of the dividers. She told us to label the little tabs of paper, fold them in half and write the heading down.

Notes, Classwork, Homework. In *Notes,* she said write inside the dividers. She said that, I swear, so I started writing on the dividers, and there was these voices rising up all at once, quiet all morning but now all up and laughing and when I looked up to see what they were laughing at it was me. I was writing on the dividers, just kept taking notes on whatever I was supposed to be taking notes on, but *on* the divider, not on the notebook paper inside the divider.

Mrs. Carter, her baby blue sweater over her t-shirt, her jeans and her white Keds. Nice the way a mom would look, like a friend's mom who thought you were a good kid that was raised properly, that's what I got out of that smile.

And she was nice about it too. "No Jay," she said. "I said to write *in* the dividers, not *on* the dividers."

Me, there, the way language went into my ear and sent messages to my brain.

"I don't think I was clear enough," she said, she couldn't hold it back at all, held out the laugh all the way to the end. "at least not clear enough for you." And there was this bell sound that was so loud it felt like it pierced my inner ear when it rang.

School went by for months like that. Walking from class to class. Mrs. Carter, and two electives, Spanish and Phys Ed.

My Spanish Teacher, Mrs. Morales, was this older lady, who was very Catholic and very concerned for our souls. She had these sayings. She got down on her knees every time she said: "Ay Dios Mio" and she'd do the three pointed neck to chest prayer for us. She told us all the time how we pushed her and pushed her until she couldn't take it anymore. Standing up and pointing a finger at a kid whose eyes were red.

"Señor," she said, "are you on mood modifiers?" She let the "-ire" in fire ring out just to see if he was high. She thought we were all in deep, deep trouble, but really, none of us were on drugs. "What you are doing is a barbarity." We had no idea what she was talking about. It's only now, years later, looking back that I know. She was talking about masturbation. All us boys, according to her, we were a barbarity, we were all chronic masturbators on mood modifiers.

And then there was Phys Ed, which was short for me, always being picked last for teams.

Don't know why the teacher had students pick their own teams.

AFTER A FEW DAYS OF being picked last. I decided on my way of handling it. Which was to wander far away from the rest of the class. Wander off and let my mind take me to faraway places.

I was lying down on the grass. It was a clear crisp late fall Miami morning, no humidity, so for once I could actually breathe. There were people playing kickball far away, but I had been left out. No one would pick me, so I decided to go off on my own. I laid right down so I could see the sky, so I could daydream, write my ticket out of there. Focus on a daydream instead of watching my body not doing what I wanted my body to do.

And the Phys Ed teacher saw me. "Pershall, get in the game," she said. And she ran over and I saw her head look down over mine, and I could tell by the wrinkles on her face and where they were how mad she was, for skipping out on the game, for daydreaming instead of doing what I was supposed to do, and she put her hand down on my shoulder and there was pain all up and down my neck, hot burn like I'd never felt before, she was there and she didn't have her hand on me and still the burn was down my neck and back. And it was then I realized I was lying on a fire ant pile. Fire ants because the feeling was fire all around my neck. And she grabbed my hand and pulled me up and walked me over to the building and everyone stopped playing the game of kickball I wasn't invited to play in and there was a burn up my neck and ears, and ass and balls and I was crying and I felt the light in my head that meant I could pass out at any time.

And the whole way back the teacher, all she could say was, "I'm sorry."

NOT ALL DAYS WERE AS bad as that though, Mrs. Carter did this thing, got me every time. Mrs. Carter stood by her normal place in the front of the classroom. By the flag.

"You know the system," she said to the class. She was one of the patient teachers. She took a long time between words. "Single file all the way to the cafeteria."

All of us stood up there, the clothes they wore all of them in shorts or skirts and light cotton t-shirts or little girl blouses, me I was still dressed for New York. Pants, belt, polo shirt tucked in tight.

"Ok, one, two, ready march." Mrs. Carter laughed like she was pretending she was a drill sergeant. Nobody else, laughed. A smile headed in my direction from Mrs. Carter when I followed the line into the hall.

There were no windows in the hallway. The clock had this mesh cage over it. Just in case any one of us wanted to toss a bottle into the clock to try and break time.

It was strange how quiet we were, for a bunch of seventh grade kids standing there in line.

NOT TALKING, WAITING TO GET into the lunchroom. And then the bell sound but closer, so loud it stretched the idea of how loud a bell could ring. The two doors opened up by a lady in a gray uniform, and a black hairnet wrapped over her big hair. The way she stood, between us and the food, like she was guarding a room full of jewels. She was a Caribbean woman, big voice, big smile. She was the only color in this hallway.

"Come on kids," she said, "Soup's on."

THE DOORS PARTED, AND WE walked in.

The room had a set of windows at the back with bars over them, the windows were so short they barely let any light in. There was swamp green tile and long rows of white tables with black edges and bright baby blue seats attached.

We moved single file into the room. Some students had brown paper bags with all varieties of sandwiches, potato chips, and the whole room smelled like oranges.

Then there was this other smell coming from the other side of the cafeteria. Like every vegetable I'd ever eaten boiled down into puke. Curved track of cafeteria that started with a big stack of trays at one end. And a long line of plastic steamed up windows, and no matter what the entree, be it chicken and dumplings or fried chicken, even the peas looked gray.

"Chicken and dumplings please." I said to the same woman who said, "Soup's on."

"Here's a little something extra for you, baby," she smiled so big, the gold fillings in her front teeth showed.

Sat down at the long table. Right in the middle, didn't know I could sit anywhere else. There was my plate with the pile of extra chicken and dumplings, these peas with all the green cooked out of them. My fork and knife, the dark khaki color to the lunch tray and a carton of orange juice.

On the carton was the state of Florida, thick green outline of the state in green and orange in the center. That orange was so bright it warmed my face. Two seats away were the voices.

"No, dude, don't do it."

"If you twist it tight enough, it will explode."

TWO BOYS, JUST A FEW seats away from me. They were twisting up a ketchup packet, twisted it so hard that when it burst, it sounded like a cap gun going off. And up on the wall was another clock that also had a cage over it, up on the clock is where all heads turned. The two boys got what they wanted, they twisted up a ketchup packet tight enough until it exploded and launched a slick red squirt up to the clock.

That ketchup on the bars over the clock. How we all waited, let time hang in the air to see if we really wanted to go through with it. This one space in time. That was the moment when all the months of "Yessir. No Sir" of standing in line ended, this was that moment for not being picked for any game on any day, this was when I hadn't yet felt the burn of those red ants. The months of oppression laid down heavy upon us, and now it was time. Three or four of us standing up, food in hand, we were, all of us, ready. One squirt of ketchup on the clock and it was game on: Food Fight!

It's easy to get lost in time. To want to stay there all the time, that there could be, for even a second, be a time when kids ruled the world. That for a full five minutes the rules didn't matter, there was no way they could overtake us. We had them outnumbered, and I was new to a new school with silent *single file walks* to the cafeteria and *I told you to take notes there and not there*. That there was even, for a second, a let up. All of this meant to me was about control.

That I could do anything I wanted to. The thing these adults feared the most was direct action.

And if I could do this here, right here at this moment. My plate up and off my tray, that cage, the idea that time needs to be caged, lifted up my plate with two hands, and even though it never came remotely close to hitting the clock, I was able to get it up and over the table we later on pushed down as a battering ram. Threw my plate with the extra chicken and dumplings with one hand and it pitched over our bunker table, hit the other long table on the other side of the lunch room turned over, bunker style, just like ours.

That lone ketchup packet, that's what started it.

Do it once and do it again and keep on doing it until Principal Cleary came in.

SHE DIDN'T HAVE TO SCREAM, the sound of the door opening was enough. That latch sound and all of us stopped, right in the middle of what we were doing. Put our arms down.

"Now clean this up," she said, "or there'll be detentions for all." She was far enough away to just be a voice. Then the door closed. And we stood there, not sure what to do next. Then it was, another shot, a cookie, black on the outside and white on the inside, smashed against the same door Principal Cleary had just closed, then it all started up again. Kids, squirted juice out of juice boxes right into other kids faces. Flanks of kids throwing potato chips and apples, smashing slow motion style against the barricade of turned down tables on either side of the lunch room. And right there at the back, the woman who gave me the extra chicken and dumplings, she had this smile to her. She loved how fast all the rules got broken.

This moment was the last of our freedom, this moment right before we stopped and went back to class and took notes in the wrong places and stood up and walked single file and shut up. And do what I tell you to do, the rest of it, going back to being kids that were ferried around by people you loved and people who left you behind.

DATING DAD

DATING DAD. THAT ANYONE would want to date Dad. That dating was a thing that Dad could do. I couldn't even see Dad love or kiss anyone else but Mom. So I was pretty fucking surprised when I saw the post it note when I came home late one night from one of my rides with Cliff. Months of no contact and all of a sudden there's a post it note.

Dinner.

7:00pm.

Cliff will drive. Love you pal, Dad.

OF COURSE I WAS STILL pissed that all of a sudden Dad wanted to spend time with me, but there was another part that came up. The Dad down in the parking garage who was rubbing my shoulders trying to make me believe that this Miami thing would fix what's broken between us. The manipulative side of Dad who always got what he wanted. No matter how much I hated him, he was my father and all he had to say was "Love you pal," and I wasn't mad at him anymore.

So it was odd how the next day just before seven pm, he wasn't around at all. Not upstairs in his office, not in his bedroom. Not on the patio.

I was in the great room that looked out onto the pool/spa area waiting for some sign from him. The books on the coffee table were all the books he had in his office in Manhattan: photo books of Roman highways, all the empires he wanted to build, all those years in his office, and how quickly we moved from one place to another. And then the all too familiar honk of Bonnie from outside.

Cliff was in the front driveway when I got up. I had switched to more nocturnal hours ever since Cliff started taking care of me. For tonight's shift, Cliff was dressed in full on limo driver's penguin suit. He stood outside holding the back door of the limo open.

Went outside, and this time, for just this one time Cliff, was holding the door open for me.

I didn't have to squeeze down into some space where I couldn't be seen.

This time, I got to ride in the back. This time, I got to be the client.

I wasn't alone back there. Dad was in the back seat too.

𝔇**AD'S ARMS WITH HIS PERFECTLY** tailored blazers on either side of the Miami Herald Newspaper with the headline *Cuban Crime Wave up 300 percent* on the cover.

Big cough from him. Dad's way of saying hi.

Dad and I were sharing space, but who we were had changed so much, so we had to play catch up. What could I say to the man who only a few months ago abandoned me to the guy who was driving us to dinner? I had to pretend that this was normal, but I hadn't seen Dad in months.

There was something about what was coming up next that made me pause. About where we were going. The person I was before would've waited for him to speak, but not now.

"Dad, where the hell are we going?" I said.

Dad put his newspaper down, his face in the back of the limo, his suit, his short hair, close shave, how tight the knot in his tie was. All the effort he took to look at Cliff or at the space just beyond my face, but never once at me.

"Oh," Dad said. And there was this huge pause where before there would be no pause. "I've been meaning to tell you," he said, "I've been seeing someone."

This someone had to be someone serious if I was meeting her. I knew Dad saw women, that was part of the reason why Cliff took care of me as much as he did.

Dad there before he spoke, not the usual tension in a box, his body, the way he sat up straight, there was no anger in him.

"Let's just say she makes me happy," Dad said, and for a second his eyes met mine. That moment, those eyes. I wasn't the only person who had changed.

The whole rest of the way there we didn't say anything. Rickenbaker causeway to Key Biscayne. We crossed one body of water just to get to dinner. He was out to impress her, I'd figured that out.

Cliff up there, even though I finally got to be the client, I missed being up there, him and me against the world. Back here the seats were more comfortable, but there was this distance, to Cliff and Dad and life in general. And then I saw wealth for what it is and what it was and what it will always be. It's the freedom of distance, from being cramped, having your own place, you don't have to share with anyone, your own stuff, and, yeah, riding in the back was everything I wanted even if Dad was right next to me, like the mini bar in the back with the soda I didn't touch. Just didn't seem right when Cliff was going to have to clean it up at the end of the night. I knew that Dad being Dad he wouldn't be going home with me, he'd go back to Nora's place like he had every night for a week or so. Which meant at the end of the night after Dad introduced me to his girlfriend, I'd be back to where I started, I'd be riding shotgun next to Cliff back to Bella Vista.

This place, this restaurant, the Rusty Pelican.

Dad and I got out of the Limo, Dad got out first of course, always first, but when I got out, he turned around and there he was, just a guy looking at his son and smiling, and yeah at the time I was still pissed about it, but really it was pretty damn ok.

Book One 1980 | Dating Dad

The front door of the Rusty Pelican was made out of the hulls of some old boats. Dad pulled open the double door, and there it was in all of its glory, crab pots and old scuba masks, big spheres with glass, so much brass inside, but also white linens, waiters in tuxedos and light soft jazz piped through the whole place, and above it all, outside, were the broken planks of wood up top that said Rusty Pelican.

Dad did that embarrassing thing he did at restaurants where he'd whistle at whoever looked official, be it waiter or busboy. If that didn't work he'd snap his fingers. He had no idea how bad it looked, Dad ordering the whole goddamned world around.

When someone did finally come and escort us back towards the window with the full view of Biscayne Bay, it was to a three-place round table, so we could see the lights coming on from the boats all around, and the lights out to the bridge going back to the Miami mainland.

On the walls were stapled relics of sea stuff, mermaids, treasure chests, crab pots, crab nets, an old sea captain made out of wood.

Me, and Dad, and the empty place setting, fork and a knife on a white table cloth. "This is Nora," Dad said, "You are going to love her."

And wouldn't you know, Nora wasn't the first woman who walked in. We had to sit through older ladies walking in, ladies that looked half dead, and then there was *the one*.

I knew she was *the one* because Dad, the way his spine held up his back and his frame, he was relaxed for the first time in like five years. But there was something about her, something to make you believe in things like people actually having the ability to glow. Her face, her hair, she had a golden air about her that threw off the rest of the fake shabbiness that was the Rusty Pelican.

This woman, some people you meet just have something about them, they wear their joy outward and that's who she was and the more I wanted to hate her, the more I realized I couldn't. She just smelled too nice. She had the kind of smile that told me she really was a happy person, that it had nothing to do with the amount of jewelry she was wearing or how much money Dad was making back then, no. You could just tell, this Nora, she was the real deal.

Dad put his hand on my shoulder, it was so obviously a put on, for show, that hand of his felt heavier than that day down in the on the highway overpass. Seeing her for the first time felt like the three of us could maybe one day turn into something.

"Jay," Dad said. For the first time since I'd known him, he wasn't in a hurry. Dad enjoyed the spaces and the breath between my name and hers. "Meet Nora. Nora, this is Jay, my son"

And for a second he even sounded proud.

THERE WAS SOMETHING ABOUT THE way Nora carried her body, her shoulders, the way her breasts pushed up and out of her black cocktail dress. She had this necklace across her chest, a necklace that looked like four stepping stones. Those stones had this slippery wet finish to them, I wanted to see for myself if they were actually wet.

There was this opening to her, a space in her life to let me in.

DAD COULDN'T JUST LET A moment be a moment. I'd just met her, and of course, he had a phone call to take. Back in the lobby. Some business call that meant once again he was leaving me alone with someone. Only this time it was someone that wanted the responsibility. And yeah, those stones above her breasts, after meeting Kiki, I had a place in my body to send those feelings to.

"Oh honey," Nora said to Dad, "that's ok, we have so much to catch up on, don't we Jay, I mean I don't even know if you have a girlfriend."

Her there, underneath crab pots and crab traps, those wet looking stones over the tops of her breasts. The glow that was a no-shit-honest-to-god glow. I didn't know if she was coming onto me, or if she was trying to be my Mom.

"I'm not here to win you over," She said. Put her hand on the empty seat next to me, signaled me to come over and sit where Dad was.

I slid over and she made a space for me, put her arm around me and pulled me in tight, those wet stones, they weren't wet, it was an illusion, a trick of the light.

"I'm not here to be your mother," she said. She looked down at me, super gentle, unlike so many others, she meant it. She meant it so much, it threw me off guard. I was here, trying not to fall for it too much, and then she goes and mentions Mom.

I'd gotten to the point then to when people mentioned Mom, I didn't get a clear picture of her in my head anymore.

"Though I'm awfully sorry about all of that," she said.

NORA, WITH BLUE EYES AND makeup and breasts going all the way up and out like they were right there, when she said it, she meant it with her whole being.

She said it took a strong person to be able to go through that. She said that's who I was, she called me a Tough Guy.

A little smile across her face. There was a little bit of a sneaky kid in her. "The thing is you need to relax."

The sound of the place, she poured a few sips of her white wine into my empty glass. The wine when I took a sip was cold and sweet and made a warm burn in my chest.

She put her hand on mine.

"What worries me the most about how you feel about your Dad," she said.

"He loves you, you know that? I know the whole him walking away from you and putting Cliff in charge of you disappoints you, and I get it. But your Dad needed room to make his business take off and that's what he's done."

This Nora, as grand as she made me feel, was going along with Dad's view of what happened. She didn't apologize for him, but by saying his side without actually living through it, she didn't really know.

What she was really saying was yes your father loves you, even though he dumped you off to someone else, it doesn't matter, you don't matter because money is more important than you are. He loves you too much to be your father.

And I had a choice to make, to speak up, or sink into this space where someone who could end up being my mother making this all seem normal, understandable even, like why wouldn't you drop your kid in the hands of a limo driver, to father and raise, in the middle of Miami, with its rising crime rates and people of the night doing questionable things with questionable people, and this Nora wanted so bad to connect with me, and at the time I thought she was warm and funny and just so sweet, but the truth was she was mainly interested in defending my Dad for what he'd done, and I had this thing living in me and no matter how sweet she was, it wasn't going to change the fact that my father had abandoned me when I needed him the most.

"You know something," I said, a little stutter at the tip of my tongue, not wanting to say the truth but needing to anyway. "He's never apologized to me, not once. He treats this whole thing like its normal."

Normal was a mirror, and I could see into it for the first time, at the person I was becoming, this darkness in me that was in that song.. I wasn't going to be a pushover anymore, not to her, not to Dad, not anyone..

I missed Mom so much right then, how close we were once for one day and now I had to look for mom in all the women I met.

I should have called Child Protective Services on Dad for what he's done, just to watch his face change. That's what I should've said, that's what I wanted to say, only I didn't know Child Protective Services was a thing back then. No, what I actually said was pretty tame, though I didn't think it was.

"What if I just called the cops and told them, what would they say about that?" Whatever it was, it still did the trick.

Nora, that glow, that reign of positivity that coursed through her veins, the color of the powder she used over her pale face, such a pale face for Miami. But something happened when I said what I said, people are people who they are until they aren't anymore.

There was a turn in her, she put her hand on top of my hand, gave it a squeeze. She was finding her feet, she was just getting started.

"You just don't see it, do you?" she said. Her eyes got close together, the calm before she'd let me have it again.

Nora and the way she held her wine glass. Her long fingers cradling the bottom, like whatever was in that glass was giving her the courage to say what she needed to say. And that's what I wanted then, something I could drink to give me the courage to say what I needed to say.

"I'm sorry about your Mom and all, there was something she was holding back. "Do you realize how much your father is risking for you?" All this, she was getting a little drunk now, waving her free hand around the restaurant.

"It's not for him," she said, "All of this is for you."

I DIDN'T NOTICE MY BREATH OR my shoulders until two hands went over my shoulders, Dad's big thick hands on me, he leaned into me, he gave me a kiss on the back of my neck. So long since he'd done anything like that. His smell, of English Leather mixed in with his old sweat smell.

"Have you told him how it's all for him?" Dad said, the front of his voice was sweet, but there was something sinister back there, the deep dark bass part that wouldn't leave me alone. This was the plan, all along. Get me alone and wine and dine me to do what he wanted me to do. This is normal.

Dad put his arm around me, pulled me in, his lips on my cheek. "Love you pal," he said.

The wine I sipped climbed up from my stomach up to my head, my brain, the arm she moved around, Dad's breath on the back of my neck.

Nora on one side, Dad with his arms around me, surrounded on both sides by liars and thieves. This was all of what I wanted, but it wasn't based on anything real.

I leaned forward, slid out of my chair and out of his arms. Crawled under the table and got out on the other side. And there they were, Nora and Dad, in the middle of the Rusty Pelican.

"You can't just decide to be a better father," I said. Me, my moment. *I'm going to turn and leave you.*

I turned around and walked away, but there was something funny about all of this, Dad and Nora, they were so fixated on each other, it was like I didn't exist. Dad and Nora. I don't know if it was time or what but they sat there staring at each other, stuck in a moment.

My moment to stand up to my father, and he didn't even notice.

WALKED BY THE TABLES OF rich people dining and drinking, the purr of soft jazz, the long picture window and the view of the bridge back to the Miami mainland, crab pots and spears, buoys, and cleats, flippers and masks.

When I pushed those double doors of the Rusty Pelican open, the chill to the air, the breeze of Biscayne Bay, there was no one out there waiting for me.

OUTSIDE

MY VIEW FROM OUTSIDE the crab-hulled double doors of the Rusty Pelican was one long ribbon of road over the Rickenbacker Causeway, and the calm of the water all the way back to the Miami Mainland. The parking lot, two street lights had these dots of bugs flying too close to the light. The sound of the lights' buzz over rows of cars and limos in the parking lot. All those cars but no Cliff and no Bonnie.

No Cliff meant no Swishers, but after the wine that Nora had just given me, a swisher just wasn't going to cut it. The idea that something liquid in a glass could change what I thought and how I thought was incredible to me. Now, I had two things if you counted the Swishers to cut out the edge I had in me back then: The 24/7 worry I felt about people and what their agendas meant for me. All along there was a way out to all of this. I could check out whenever I wanted. I got to make the call.

By drinking or inhaling in one reality and exhaling out another I could become someone older, wiser, more fucked up and distant. I could become liquid, I could become smoke.

I didn't have any more time to think about it, because Cliff came roaring up into the parking lot.

The smell of meatball parmesan sandwiches hit me right off when I walked up and opened the door, my door, Meatball Parms, two of them. One for Cliff and One in the passenger seat waiting for me.

"Figured I'd order you some real food." Cliff said. Cliff already had tomato sauce on his chin, he had a square of greasy napkin folded he rubbed over the same patch of scruff on his face, a place he forgot to shave.

And here's the kind of bastard I was. Here Cliff knew what was up, knew at some point that I'd get fed up and want to leave early and though it would be nice to stop and pick up some food, not just any food, this was Miami Subs, this was *our* food. And Cliff, he was going to take me home and come back to get Dad and Nora. He did all this for me.

But I didn't care about any of that. I see it now, the asshole that I was. Because I had one thing on my mind and one thing only.

A bottle in our fridge at home. Chilled like the little bit I had inside the Rusty Pelican.

White wine in our fridge, a whole bottle of it, probably the exact same kind that Nora had given me inside the Pelican. Nora was in our life and so was our wine.

I was out of Swishers too, which meant I had to steal more, from Cliff.

All of this was the part of me that was growing bigger every day, the little bit of dark that burned everything else out.

Me, what I did was steal two swishers right in front of Cliff. I did my finger trick, pointed to the hammerhead display shark in front of the Miami Seaquarium that spun around even though he was a part of a sign above ground, not in the water. It was our thing to laugh at.

So we did, we laughed.

And I slid two swishers out of the open pack in cup holders between us.

Some nights when I stole them I could see things I couldn't have seen. My imagination filled in what my brain didn't know. I could see things that weren't there, like Cliff knowing full well I'd stolen Swishers that I'd been stealing for days, weeks even. But what could he do but sit there and play this hammerhead shark game with me.

Slid them into my pocket. Two of them, enough for tonight, when I got home.

And that's the thing, what the whole ride home was, was actually a great night, one of the best with Cliff, but I didn't enjoy any of it. I was too busy waiting to get home so I could tear into that wine that Nora kept in our house.

Before tonight I didn't know anything about Nora or the wine she kept. I figured it was Dad's when I saw it in our fridge, but there we were Cliff and I, rounding the corner onto Bella Vista. Down that two-lane road with palm trees straight down the middle all the way to the ocean, to Mar Street.

And getting out of the limo. Cliff, he just had to say it, he still clung on to the idea that I was a kid that needed looking after, that at thirteen I wasn't someone becoming older, someone old enough to steal booze and steal smokes that I was going to go enjoy right after I got out of the car.

The humidity slapped me in the face like it always did, the sudden change of AC to that marshy salt smell, and it hit me where my stomach met my heart, that space in my chest and what I was about to do. Sometimes it took something like smelling the marshy salty-ass mangroves to tell me just how much I'd grown up on this one evening. And Cliff had no idea about this thing growing in me, or if he did he didn't let on, because he did his thing, waves his wand a little bit at me, and started the engine.

"Good night, sweet prince," he said.

His face there in the light of our driveway, white, fluorescent glow on his chin, after all that wiping, he still had a little bit of tomato sauce on his chin.

I went inside. Locked the door. Put my shoes away where I was supposed to. Opened up the fridge, there it was: the Bottle. Chilled white wine. It still had the cork sticking out, I didn't have to know how to work a corkscrew. There wasn't much more than a splash, maybe half a glass, if I was being generous. But what did I know? It all went into a plastic kid cup, the kind Dad would prefer me to use, just in case I dropped the glass on the floor and fucked something else up.

The sound it made went into my green plastic cup. The one from the pizza place back in Brooklyn, the kind of place you would take a family, back when I still had a family. I went out the sliding glass door by the room with the couches and the tall ceilings.

OUTSIDE, THERE WAS A SLIGHT wind. I got out the lighter that was in the odds and ends drawer in the kitchen. That lighter, the rough edge of it on my thumb when I lit up a Swisher. A smoke in one hand and a green plastic cup half full of cold white wine..

That first sip. There's controlling destiny and then there's controlling destiny, this sip I got, I earned, how I had to wait awhile for it. And give up the one person who actually cared about me. Me, there, breathing in stolen smoke, sips of stolen wine. I was hijacking my way into a new personality, making new out of old, destroying the little boy who needed a father or a mother, I was different now, I breathed in a new life for myself.

There was a chill in the sip of white wine I took. How quick the chill in me went away. I was one person and now I was another. Because there was warmth in my chest that spread out to the rest of me, from my chest to my throat, from my throat to my head, to the rest of me, breathe in and it's dark inside, breathe out and I'm looking out to the canal, the shapes of masts and boat lines, triangles and tips.

Book Two 1987 | Outside

DURING MY FIRST FEW months in Miami I was still holding on to all the things I still had when I lived in Park Slope. Like having two parents, at least one who stayed straight throughout the day, who wasn't stoned or high on coke.

Most people learn about drug addiction and parental abandonment in books, but I had to see mom on her knees, begging for the next hit. When she was around making me a sandwich, or when it was just the two of us folding laundry together, no matter where we were, or what we were doing, when we were together, she wasn't really there.

We had that one afternoon of her painting me on that stool, and we had the in-between moments where she'd put her hand on my cheek and just sort of leave it there. Or she'd rub the top part of where my cheek starts. Always with the cheeks, and her hand on my head. To her my head must've been a Buddha belly.

Which is a long way of saying that without anyone else around, Cliff had become kind of a parent to me. But I couldn't appreciate it, the thing that lived in me, what I now called my "Little Friend," made me drive a wedge between the only person who cared about me.

The end had been coming for a while. I was old enough to take care of myself. There was a bus stop down by the construction site, up to where the tree-lined median strip started where Bella Vista started that would take me to school.

Cliff wanted the best for me even if he had to drive me around in the middle of this fucked up time in the history of the universe to do it, even if our rides only happened once a week. Dad wasn't paying him for it anymore. My plan, but really my friend's plan was to keep stealing Swishers until I could pass for eighteen. If Cliff didn't catch me. All this time and somehow I hadn't been caught. Some nights when I was up late smoking one of them, outside with a little chilled white wine, I'd imagine Cliff knowing all along that I'd been stealing.

Hadn't seen Cliff in a while and one night when I sat down in the limo and there was a carton there.

A carton.

10 packs of 5 Swishers each. In a box.

On the seat.

The carton, those ten packs of Swishers, they weren't just a gift, shit, I still wasn't old enough to smoke, no, this was a kind of intervention, this was a test, to see just how much I'd been stealing. That's what I guessed, especially with the way Cliff was holding his body, straight up and down, ten and two on the wheel.

Cliff had his chin jutted out, and his attention was deadlocked on me.

"**L**OOK," **HE SAID. "IF YOU'RE** looking for a friend then cool. Because that's what I want," he said. "Or if you're in it just for stealing my smokes then go ahead and take the carton now."

Cliff, I'd never heard him that angry before. And even though my Little Friend had done this, I still felt the sick of my stomach crawl up to my throat.

I had made the only person who cared about me mad enough to sit up and tell me about it.

"**C**LIFF," I SAID. I TRIED to make peace. I didn't want to just take advantage of the guy, I hadn't gotten that hard, yet.

He cut me off. 'I don't want to hear any fake apologies."

CLIFF HAD HIS LIMO CAP on and there were tufts of his dark brown hair with a slight orange tint when the sunlight hit it just right.

"I've been kind," he said, held out a finger for each laundry list of things I owed him. "I've been there for you in all kinds of situations. Shit's fucked up, but in my job shit is always fucked up. That doesn't mean you can steal from me."

That face of his all tight, that posture. What he was looking for was an apology, or at the very least to look like maybe I gave a shit about him enough to feel bad, a frown so he saw I felt sorry for him.

I wasn't having any of this.

"Are you saying you would've given me smokes when I was 11?" I said. I didn't just touch his nerve, I pounced all over it.

"You could've asked," Cliff said. "You could've started a conversation."

"I do a lot of good for a lot of fucked up people," Cliff said, "If it's one thing I've learned, it's not to judge, everyone's got shit they're ashamed of.

"And besides," he said. "You're sixteen now not eleven."

The Cliff there on that day, was the same of Cliff as any other day. Was part of why I loved him so much: he never judged.

He said, "We all make mistakes. This much I know."

The look on his face, I knew he couldn't stay pissed at me for long. "So whaddaya say, you wanna make nice?"

Cliff knew me, or at least I thought he knew me. Maybe Cliff did what so many other people did back then, they underestimated me. Cliff forgot that I had opinions and motivations too, when I had this dark thing hovering over me, Cliff leaving himself wide open vulnerable. I saw the opening and went for it.

Cliff, The carton of smokes he bought, he put this all on me. The only thing was, as much as I wanted to have an adult actually care about me, there was that other thing, my Little Friend was now calling the shots, in a way he always had.

"Look," I said. I don't know where I found the words or the clarity or the balls, but I said it. Stepped back and let out all that pissed off out of me. The mood I got in, when my friend came, there was this far away distance to everything, especially those closest to me, this tired feeling at the front of my head, like I could pass out at any moment.

"I don't know if you know this," I said. "But I'm not your son, so let's stop pretending that I am."

I knew what my friend's plan was, and I felt the sickness in my stomach turn to sour. "I love you," I said. "But I'm going through something you haven't."

And right then, Cliff's whole chin-forward game was gone. His eyes, that posture of his, he was back to being a broken human being again.

"You could've tried me, kid."

"You don't get it," I said. I felt like I knew enough about what was going on in me that I could finally talk about it. "Half the time the things I say aren't me." I said, "I'm not a nice guy when I get this way. I can't tell the difference between the two of them or us, or whoever, It's like I got this other kid inside of me, and he's calling the shots."

For the first time I felt like it was ok to talk about what was really happening. And I thought Cliff was going to understand too

"I'm sorry I stole from you," I said. "And at the same time I'm not." Cliff looked up at me. Took his time, I could tell, he'd been crying.

"Look kid," he said. "Loyalty is kind of a big thing for me and you are obviously old enough to look after yourself."

Cliff, wrapped his hand around my arm, pulled me in close. "It's time, kid, that's what you need," Cliff said.

He let go of my arm, slid his palm up on my arm, pushing me out of Bonnie as slow as he could.

"You need time to figure this out, so that's what I'm going to give you. You take your time, and you come back."

He had me halfway pushed off my seat. He picked up the carton, put it on my lap. The lapels, his cufflinks.

"I'm in a little over my head here, I'll pay for your smokes."

CLIFF HELD THAT BUSINESS CARD of his so close to me I couldn't see anything else, couldn't see why the card was shaking or how he was probably crying behind that business card with his number on it.

"Call me when you know who you are again," he said.

THAT NUMBER, THAT BUSINESS CARD was my last chance and I didn't take it. I didn't take the card, I didn't take down the number, I opened the door, I slid the rest of the way out of my seat, got back out on my driveway, and went inside.

Cliff was done with me.

ALL THOSE WORDS AND IDEAS and finally I had a way to talk about them, but no one to understand this new language. It didn't matter how clearly I got my point across, Cliff's world was black and white, all or nothing.

Growing up where Cliff grew up, New York, being crazy or depressed or sad all the time just wasn't acceptable. In his mind life was a job, you have a bad day, you go home and drink a few beers and go to sleep and the next day you put on your suit and you go to work and you live another day.

Me, I was out of the picture.

Bella Vista

ALONE

THAT NEXT DAY, THE part of me that made me leave Cliff was nowhere to be found. It was morning, and I felt bad about what I did to him, felt bad for not going to school, and felt bad for not using my trusted out BMX bike to get there.

There was only one thing that was going to make me feel better.

I DID WHAT I DID WHENEVER I was alone back then, I got onto Dad's boat, got the gold colored padlock heavy in my hand, slid the dials up and down to line up to what I knew to be the combination. Walked down the steps of the ladder down into the kitchen, pulled up the metal handle of the fridge, reached down into where the beers were.

With my headphones on, my Walkman moved me through the songs I'd taped off of college radio, so the music was all over the place: dirges and metal, punk and no less than one thousand sad songs.

Walked through the side yard out to the front, onto the street.

The first sip, cold beer down my throat, the feeling of being loved that comes from a bottle.

I had my beer and lit up a swisher, I was complete.

A FEW HOUSES DOWN, ON BELLA Vista I saw a little bit of space between the trees. A break in the mangroves. Dried mud crawling to the right, a spot of solid ground to put my feet on, a path back there.

Only a few steps in and already there was all kinds of mischief: the burnt-out edges of a twelve pack of the worst beer imaginable, empty cigarette packs, pink underwear, a black bra on a branch. There was a log, a place where people could drink and take off each other's clothes.

I sat down on the log, took one last drag of my swisher, drank what was left of the beer.

THESE TWO THINGS, A BIT of feeling in my chest I felt that for a second, that maybe, things were going to be ok.

Put out the swisher in the bottle. Headed down the path curved around alternating sets of woods and mangroves. Sun peeking through the trees and a light feeling in my chest where normally I wouldn't be able to breathe. I walked for a while, starting to feel something else, further away, farther out than I thought this whole mangrove system went, and then there was this dip down back down into brown twigs, salty marsh, mangroves.

Above me, the sun was always there but now it was an overhang of branches and leaves, far enough down the path to where I couldn't hear the traffic anymore. Just my feet sloshing through the mud and the muck, the smell, that salt water everywhere smell was so strong I could taste it at the back of my throat.

There was some kind of a click in there, a bird stepping on a stick, or a frog that shook a leaf, maybe the part of me that was still a kid thought the noise I was hearing was an alligator.

When I stopped, my feet were in the brown brackish water. The stink of salt marsh all over me. Hot too.

I was all alone out here.

NORMALLY I WOULD'VE TURNED AROUND and went home. But I didn't. I was going to keep walking for as long as it took me to find what I was looking for.

The path picked back up, gaining more ground, then up the hill a bit, the path cleared, then water, but much larger on the other side of the trees. Some kind of a pond back there.

A pond in the middle of the mangroves, so big it even had a little island in the center.

THE THINGS I SAW NEXT, how could my eyes send messages to the brain fast enough to process as much as I saw when I turned a corner and the mangroves became a clearing.

The scene in front of me, a view that changed when I turned around the corner to all that water, a pond. And a canoe and tools, rope and a cart, and two boys standing there.

Two boys, one real tall, the other kind of short. Both with cigarettes going. Two stooges skipping school, just like me. One of them looked like he went to school all the time, the other looked like he hadn't been in years.

These two, Caleb and Bryan, or the Psycho and Beat-Your-Ass Bryan, as I would later call them. Beat-Your-Ass Bryan because if someone looked at him for too long, his lazy eye wouldn't like it and he'd beat your ass. These two didn't stay at home when they skipped school, they lived in the nooks and crannies of the mangroves.

Caleb had these bright blue eyes for girls to fall in love and a preppy look to match: Polo shirt buttoned up, tucked in, slacks. I'd never seen anyone quite that psychopathic before. He could play the innocent kid to perfection. One flash of those baby blues and any parent would trust him. And when their backs were turned, that's when the knife went in.

Bryan wore green military camo gear. He had this blonde mullet, Bryan with his long hair hung down over his stupid face. His headphones always had some hair metal band playing through them. Even with all that, I was still more comfortable with him than with Caleb. He was a dumbass but at least he was my dumbass.

The two of them kept busy: they drank beer, they drank vodka, they climbed trees and made bonfires. They gave each other tattoo smiley faces with the hot end of a lighter. Most of the time, when people make friends, it's because of something they share. And that's what happened, I liked these two exactly because they were being dumb and dangerous on purpose, like that was the point.

I was hanging with kids that only a year ago would've kicked my ass.

How different I could be if I wanted to. Something about me had to change. If I carried on being as sensitive and caring as I was, I would've gotten killed. That's how serious I took it, life or death, fight or flight.

And maybe it was this dark path, Deadbird Redbird or the long lineage line from me to my father to my father's father. I was tired of playing the victim and, with Caleb and Bryan, I could start over.

So when I introduced myself to these two, I didn't do it the way I would've even a year or two earlier. I hit them before they could hit me. Walked over and punched them in the arm. One then the other, like it was a handshake.

The moment before was a history I could rewrite. Start brand new. Start by hitting, punching, kicking, whatever it takes to be who I wasn't before.

Because I could be someone who could just walk up and hit someone. I mean I couldn't until I started to listen to the little guy who was now calling the shots. But all this wasn't for nothing. It was my way of saying me and Caleb and Bryan; we're the same.

After I hit Caleb, after I hit Bryan there was this huge pause where the water from the pond rippled with the wind.

Caleb pulled up his sleeve to show me his tattoo, two blisters for eyes from the part of the lighter you flick with your thumb and the swoop of the smile from the part of the lighter where the flames come out.

"We, the two of us, back here." Caleb said, "We're marked," he said that if I was one of them I'd do it too.

Said the vodka would give me the courage.

THE VODKA WAS THE CHEAP kind, in a small plastic flask that had a big reindeer on it. Came out of Bryan's green trench coat. All Caleb had to do was say the word.

The bottle, small, red and silver, and black, the colors of Soviet Russia. The first sip burned like I was drinking the stuff Mom used to rub on my arm when I scraped it. After a few sips the Vodka went one step beyond my usual buzz, the Vodka scooped out the last bit of nervous I felt hanging with these two.

Bryan's stupid face, his stupid smile.

BRYAN TOOK HIS STUPID HAND and wrapped it around the top of my arm, so Caleb could burn a tattoo there.

Bryan held me down and Caleb held the hot metal on my right shoulder. It hurt like a sonofabitch, but that wasn't as bad as It could've been. I did have the vodka. Felt good enough going down to where I didn't feel the twin blisters for eyes from the metal spark wheel, or the burn from the curl in the shape of a smile from where the flame came.

The three of us back in those mangroves, we were a team.

THEY HAD THIS METAL CART with wheels and a big old handle, sitting in the three or four feet of the pond, trying to stay cold was a case of beer, the worst beer imaginable, the beer the beer aisle starts with.

Caleb's eyes did that thing they did where it looked as if those eyes of his took up half of his face, and fuck if it didn't make me feel that much closer to being dead than I already did.

"Stole this from my Dad," he said, "I used his credit card."

CALEB, WHEN HE SAID THAT, he was testing to see just how far I was willing to take this thing. There was a whole what-do-you-think-about-that in the way he said it, drawing attention to himself, absolutely requiring your respect. Caleb had power.

And I laughed because that's what I would've done. I Took the one thing my Dad had over me and turned it against him. And the way I was headed, it wasn't going to be much further before I was gonna get a chance to do that.

"I was inside this convenience store," Caleb said. "One of those drive through ones," he looked at us like we didn't know the whole story and we would have to just sit there and wait until he was done.

"And I'm driving the car and this guy comes over to the car like they always do, and he's ready to ID me, So I told the guy I knew things about his wife, I knew her name, don't ask me how I knew her name, but I did. And I got the beer."

"And the best part," Caleb said, "Is that my Dad's a recovering alcoholic."

He was standing over by the case. He tossed one to me, he tossed one to Bryan. "Cheers to him," he said.

Me and Bryan, we pretended like we didn't hear him, we were all about one and then another and another. We cracked open a third.

And somehow, the tattoos, the bullshit, and without saying a word, we knew how similar we were. We hated everyone else, or at least they did. Either way, we needed each other. It was gonna get worse before it got better.

"I know your pop is rich," Caleb said to me. Those eyes of his were already in on a plan I didn't know about yet.

"Rich, shit." Caleb said, he had this look on his face, there was a plan forming, a need, if only he had the full lineup of what was there for the taking.

"What kind of rich shit does he got?"

ILL GOTTEN GAINS

RICH. SHIT. **CALEB, WHEN** Caleb said that. I knew he was capable, but I didn't know he'd actually broken into a bunch of houses in the neighborhood. He spent evenings looking up into the lights on in the windows, or at a dark house. His mind was always taking notes. He couldn't help it. He loved to steal.

He didn't need to. His Dad had his own store, boat parts. But all those things he had access to, the rope and flares, ladders and hooks, were the things he needed to steal.

Caleb saw burglary as a problem to figure out. He cased every house he broke into. He was so elegant, he wore surgical gloves so he wouldn't leave any fingerprints. A cat burglar in the old sense. Caleb got to know the patterns of coming and going of the residents of these houses: Moms and Dads and lawyers and divorce, pickup and drop off. He knew when they went to bed and he knew when they left the house for work in the morning. Whether it was in the middle of the afternoon or the middle of the night Caleb knew the perfect time to break in.

Of course I didn't know any of this when the three of us sat around a campfire by the pond, drunk on vodka, my left arm sore from the hot metal that had been pushed against it a few hours earlier. Because I could see the plan forming in Caleb's head if I couldn't quite see it on my own.

THE COMING TOGETHER OF HOW me and Caleb would break into Dad's house, my house, and pretend it was some burglary. Caleb had it all covered.

What he called Standard Operating Procedure. He laid out the plan by the pond, a few nights later, the three of us and a fire.

He had a map of the entire neighborhood. He was standing up, between the two of us. Pointing at the house at the end of the canal, the one with the red ballpoint circle drawn around it. He had a beer in one hand, sat down on one of two long logs.

"They can't find you if you weren't ever there," he said.

And I felt it just then, the difference between being an older person and being a kid.

THERE ARE DECISIONS WE MAKE, where after we make them we change who we are. After I did this, I couldn't go back.

And it wasn't just me being pissed off, there was the warm I got from the beer, and the always another and another and another. I'd gone too far to come back.

I knew the good kid I used to be was going away, but each time I thought about it, I used the beer or the vodka or the Swisher, or whatever was in front of me, to push away that thinking.

"Oh you know," I said, finally answering Caleb's question. "The usual rich stuff, some jewelry, an insane stereo system he only uses to listen to classical."

The rest of the house, up the stairs, he had his papers, the cabinet Dad was always real sure I didn't go anywhere near.

"He's got this cabinet in his office that probably has some serious cash or something stashed inside that I'm not even allowed to see," I said. And when I said it, I was glad I did.

That cabinet, I knew that cabinet had something in it. Had to be some kind of serious injection of funds for Dad to buy something like Bella Vista so quick. He hadn't even stepped into the house before he bought it.

"Don't know what's in it," I said, "but he's always careful about locking it."

I DIDN'T KNOW IF DAD WAS crooked, and I didn't know dick about international finance, I knew that us being as rich as we were all of a sudden was about as non-existent as the quality of parenting he'd been providing ever since we pulled away from our house in Park Slope and moved to Bella Vista.

"That's good," Caleb said, "we'll start there."

DIRTY DEEDS

BELLA VISTA, BEAUTIFUL VIEW, a place so beautiful but empty. On the inside, there was hardly any furniture and what there was felt far away and modern, distant. Inside was money and wealth and no heart behind it. We had the house but we didn't have a family.

And there was something about that cabinet I had to know about. The more I thought about it the more I realized that whatever was inside would tell the truth about how we got everything so quick, without even selling the house in Park Slope.

What was inside that cabinet became an obsession? A thing I had to find.

I DON'T KNOW WHAT I WAS expecting, but we had the whole thing planned out, well actually it was Caleb who had it planned out.

"Your Dad's place is actually harder to case than most," he said, which did creep me out a little, given the fact that he had been casing my house for as long as he could. Psycho kid with his buttoned-up polo shirt in the middle of the night, trying to figure out when people came home. But then, he had the mangroves to stay in, so he could watch the whole street without setting a foot on the actual pavement. He'd sit up and wait for the lights to come on, all night if he had to.

"Your Dad isn't home enough to figure out," he said. "Some days he's gone for days and then he's home every night for a week. Sometimes the lights are on but nobody's home. And that limo guy doesn't come by anymore."

Caleb just up and knowing my whole story like that, like my whole life, like the gory details were just floating in the air and all you had to do was listen hard enough to grab them.

"How long have you been doing this?" I said. Even with everything in me, I was pissed.

"I told you," he said. "I notice things, it's like a puzzle I get to figure out. It's only when I've done it, when I'm inside the house, it's only then do I understand it."

"Swear to god," I said, "you're such a fucking psycho."

Caleb stopped what he was doing, the plan, he put the map down, put his hand on my shoulder. "At least you'll get to finally figure out what's inside that cabinet."

DONE DIRT CHEAP

THE MORNING WE CHOSE for the break in, Dad had some appointment. He had it written on his big desk calendar. Dad's handwriting, in mechanical pencil.

10 AM, Vink.

THIS JOB WE WERE ABOUT to do couldn't look like an inside job. I wasn't psycho enough to break into the one locked cabinet, I needed Caleb to do that.

I couldn't ask Dad what the deal was with the cabinet. He'd lie like he lied about everything else.

Bryan, you know why we didn't bring him. Not only was he slow, we weren't sure at the end of the day that we wouldn't end up getting our asses beat for reasons not disclosed.

And plans were all well and good, but now we were here, Caleb and I outside Dad's master bedroom window. The window was between the tennis court and the canal, covered up by bushes. The window was too high up for us to get access to.

Which meant Caleb had to be taller. Which meant I had to be the stool.

I got down on my hands and knees, my hands in dirt and the heat of humidity and the smell of salt. I was just tall enough to where Caleb could reach the screen over the window when he put his flat docksider down onto the center of my back, lifted himself up and stood up both feet on my back.

He knew exactly how much force to pry up the metal screen, enough to slide in a finger or two.

On my hands and knees, I didn't see any of it. But Caleb talked me through the whole thing.

"Two fingers, and pull," he said, "Then you've got to cut the wires connected to it." Once he had the cords cut he could rip that screen off the wall and toss it.

"But not too hard, it's got to look normal when we put it back." he said.

"There's this sensor on the window, looks like a Lego brick turned on its side, with two wires sticking out of it."

Caleb had this crazy utility belt, construction worker get up, the white hard hat. "Cut those wires and then we can smash the glass."

I turned to look up and saw he had one of those large rubber mallets in his hand.

"You want to break as little glass as possible," he said. "The hole needs to be big enough to open the window."

"One tap," he said, "and we're in."

Caleb standing on my back wasn't that heavy at first, but by the end, my back could barely hold him up.

The crash of mallet to glass, a moment I couldn't undo.

CALEB WITH HIS HAND THROUGH the hole in the glass. There was a flick sound, the pop of the window unlocked, the swish when he lifted up the window. Big enough so he could crawl through. I arched my back against his foot, tall enough to where Caleb could leap in.

Cocked my head around and his feet were up in the air, his body in through the window. "Meet you in front," he called out to me.

How strange of a walk it was, the dizzy head feeling from straining my back to get Caleb up, and the reason why. We weren't kids playing on the playground. We were teenagers about to become adults, and I was helping him to break into my own goddamned house in the middle of the afternoon. There I was, through the gate, by the pool, walked around to the front.

By now you are probably wondering why I didn't just let him in, why break in at all?

WHAT I WANTED WAS TO invade Dad the way he invaded me. I wanted him to feel that there was someone out there that knew he was hiding something and that person was willing to smash glass to see it. I wanted him to know but not know that his son had to do this in order to see what he was hiding from his own son.

I didn't open the front door, even though I had a key. My hand on the key in my sweaty little pocket. My fist closing down over its hard edges.

Caleb there, the look on his face, this was the only time he looked like he had life figured out.

He opened the door like he was doing me a favor. "Why do it yourself when somebody else can do it for you?"

It did feel weird walking through a house I just helped a guy break into, but all I cared about was finding out what was in that cabinet.

My steps were a few steps behind him going up the stairs, his boat shoes, pressed khaki so light they were almost white. Tucked in a blue and green striped Polo shirt just in case Dad came home. Caleb would look like a normal kid until Dad saw the hole in the window.

The squeak the stairs made whenever I was doing something I wasn't supposed to. Caleb marched up the stairs to the room next to mine, Dad's office.

The cabinet. A locked drawer as part of Dad's desk. Not one lock but two. One on the front and one on the side where the chair slid in.

Caleb slipped his gloves on, and with white surgical gloves he slipped through the first lock, the one on the front, big brass fixture with room for a key to slide through. And the way he did it, how fast he did it, like the act of breaking into it was a fact he stored somewhere, brought up and used and tossed away.

The second lock was towards the back of the cabinet. He had to pull out Dad's chair and crawl under it. He had to bring out a set of tools that looked like a sunglass kit, with all kinds of sizes I'd never seen before. Caleb pulled out two long skinny twigs made out of metal.

Took a lot of squirming to get through, but something sharp pointed to something else sharp, and then it opened, that cabinet with the two locks, the one in Dad's office with a view of the two boat cranes on the black edges of the seawall.

"Time to solve a mystery," he said. He was squinting, he could barely see through all the sweat in his eyes.

And when Caleb pulled that thing forward, there was the reflection of the two of us on the surface of a black plastic bag. One of those lawn and leaf bags I used to rake leaves back in Park Slope.

Big bag with a yellow handle all twisted up.

Me, I didn't touch it. I hadn't worn gloves like Caleb had. I kept my sweaty hands in my sweaty pockets, sweating on the key I didn't use to get in.

"Go time," Caleb said, and when he twisted it, he did this whistle that he'd seen old cat burglars do in old black and white movies. Because what was on the other side of the yellow twisted handle was green and white and green and white and green and white and numbers and presidents.

Cash, thousands of it, in a black lawn and leaf bag.

Most thieves I'd seen on TV would've gotten so crazed about seeing so much cash stored in one place that they'd lose all sense.

But not Caleb.

AFTER HE'D UNLOCKED IT. THE cabinet was open, not a scuff mark on the wood by the lock, no scrape or scratch on the brass fixture. Nothing to indicate to anyone that anything was out of the ordinary.

"The funny thing is, we can't take it all," he said. "Most people would, and they'd go to prison. But you and I, we're only taking what we need, three hundred or so, enough so we know we were here but your Dad never will."

Caleb probably thought I was thinking about all the beer and smokes three hundred dollars could buy, but me, I didn't even care about the money. Or I did, but not in the way Caleb thought I did.

Dad, this money wasn't his. I had no earthly idea whose it was, but Dad and I, we were in debt to somebody. I knew, and Dad knew, but he had no idea I knew. He wouldn't even notice it was gone.

Stack after stack after stack, thousands of dollars, probably twenty grand is what Caleb figured. Someone had the cash in a goddamned garbage bag and now it was Dad's.

And I was going to have to ask him about it.

ONLY I COULDN'T JUST COME out and ask him about the cash, but I could ask about the house, about how we got all of this Bella Vista so quickly.

Caleb wasn't going to leave without giving me a little bit of advice..

Hey man," he said, "you were good today, and you and me, we're cool, but you gotta get some help."

"Help?" I said. I couldn't focus. I was too busy staring at all that money and how none of it was ours.

"You know, a therapist, someone who can make you feel good."

Caleb had a few of those hundreds in his hand, and he handed me three of them. Three hundred dollars of my Dad's money.

"Think about it," he said.

Bella Vista

TIME TO TALK

HOW DO YOU UNSEE what you've seen? How do you walk into an office that only a few hours before you'd helped a friend break into and act like everything about this was normal?

Dad knew about the missing money the whole time. He couldn't say anything about the twenty grand of cash in a lawn and leaf bag that now was more like 19,400 after me and Caleb stole six hundred dollars. The who and why of how Dad got the money was what I was here for. Which was why I went upstairs when I knew Dad would be home, on a school day, when I hadn't seen him in what felt like months.

I knew Dad was upstairs because the stereo was on downstairs and Vivaldi's *Four Seasons*, was playing, which is what Dad was always listening to. I didn't know shit about classical music but I could pick out the rolls of violin from downstairs, *Four Seasons* covering up the squeak of the carpet on top of metal stairs.

In his office Dad had on reading glasses that pointed down to the ledger on his desk.

This was perfect timing. But how was I going to ask Dad how thousands of dollars of someone else's money ended up in a lawn and leaf bag in his office?

Right away when he saw me, Dad did his sigh thing, a sharp stream of air came out of his mouth. He sat back and sniffed the air, and started coughing. It was amazing to me that he ever managed to smoke pot.

"Why do you smell like smoke?" Dad said.

I thought we'd been over the whole smoking thing. "You know I smoke Dad."

Dad had fifteen different ways to show he was angry at me. "Aren't you supposed to be in school," he said.

Already, I had the sentence ready, a sentence that was really an act. "Yeah I know, I haven't gone in a while," I said, "I'll sort it out soon."

I might've changed, but Dad was going back to his scream until he was red in the face and his veins stuck out the side of his neck, his stock in trade, his golden oldies.

"You'll do it sooner than soon," he said. "You'll do it now."

THE OLD ME WOULD'VE BUCKLED, would've turned me back into all yessir nossir, but now that I'd seen the truth, nothing could hold me back.

"Let's talk about you for a second, Dad." He owed me an explanation, not the other way around.

"I've got to work," he said. He stood up, closed the big green ledger with his pencil marks. Took the papers that were on his desk and tapped them into a pile.

"I don't have time."

Dad was trying to wiggle his way out of this.

"Then I'll make it quick. How did we get this house so fast?"

HE DID A THING THAT would have ended the conversation full stop a few years ago. He stepped towards me, and I didn't move, I didn't back down.

Kept on with my questions, told him how we bought this house before we even sold our old house. Dad was there, hitting every question I had back to me.

"That's because your mother was living in it," Dad said.

I told him how we weren't rich, asked him: "What, they just gave you a house?"

"It's more of a loan," Dad said.

I asked Dad what we had to pay it back with, our lives?

"**L**ET'S NOT GET DRAMATIC ABOUT this," Dad said. His salesman self was taking over. "Let's just say it's a loan and I'm working on paying it back." As if this was a normal business practice.

I didn't give up, I kept pushing. I asked him what kind of bank gave away free houses. "Well it's not exactly a bank," He said. And there it was, the direct line from Dad to the money and where it came from.

"So who are we talking about here Dad," I said.

Dad there, in that moment, the long line of his accomplishments, his plan, the one he laid out to me in the parking garage all those years ago, the tapes I hid or tried to hide, the way I got caught and how that made the whole thing between Mom and Dad blow up, destroyed a family and brought us this new house, this new life, this Bella Vista, a new life that was more like a new death.

This money, and the answer, Dad's answer, instead of clearing things up, it just made things worse. Dad wasn't the only person who'd done something he couldn't undue.

And then I saw it, one word, a first name with no last name scratched out in Dad's handwriting, the meeting dad had the day Caleb and I broke in.

Vink.

I knew how to play it cool, say the name and watch Dad's face, how it would or would not change.

"The reason we have all this stuff is because of Vink, Dad, isn't it?" Dad there, in his suit and tie, so much confidence and so much of it came from having the money.

Dad, if being guilty was a process, he went straight to it, the full body muscles tight, his big body standing strong, and he was about ready to drop deep down and let me have it.

But he didn't.

I stood there, not moving at all, meeting his look, taking as much as he could give.

AND WOULDN'T YOU KNOW, THE torso of muscle Dad, the stand-your-ground Dad, the slightly tanned look to his skin, went away, he was old, pale and scared. I saw it all there, fall away.

Dad there, always with the right thing to say, whatever it took for me for you to buy whatever he was selling.

"How'd you know?" he said.

"It's written on your desk calendar."

My whole life Dad was there pulling the strings. He rose up from the stoner cloud of the Dirty Hippie and took life by the reins, and now I was the one telling him what I thought.

"I told you I had to work," he said. The way he said it, he didn't have the edge anymore. I had figured him out.

And I might've felt good for a while, felt vindicated, like this whole me and Caleb breaking into the house thing was justified, but that's the problem with being young and thinking you're right, because I didn't feel this way for long.

TOOK A FEW DAYS FOR it to really land on me. Dad was crooked and there was nothing I could do about it.

No matter what I did, he wouldn't be there to see it. I'd broken into the house and it didn't really matter. Dad saw Nora, he was never home. I'd stolen beer and wine. And he didn't say shit.

The battle with him was over.

So some weirdo-slash- possible drug dealer gave Dad twenty grand in a bag. What was I going to do about it? All Dad wanted was for me to go back to school. And right then, walking out, I didn't know why, but all I wanted to do was listen to him.

I forgot about Caleb and Bryan, who weren't my friends anyway. I didn't have a fight with them, I just stopped going to the mangroves.

I stopped drinking so much. I'd try normal, or my version of it anyway. I didn't want Cliff to take me to school, so I rode the old, trashed BMX. I liked it, feeling more like a kid, even at 16.

That dark part in me that started all of it, once I saw Dad just fall apart in front of me, the feeling went away with Dad's loss of strength, I had done it, I had changed.

WHEN SWISHERS AREN'T ENOUGH

I STILL SMOKED, EVEN DRANK a little too. But only at night when it got dark. I sat out by the seawall between the two white cranes that held boats up when they were in use. I watched the lights on the masts shine out like stars I could reach.

Only thing was, I didn't have anyone to enjoy this view with. I'd pushed away the only person who cared about me.

It was time to do it, to call Cliff, and apologize.

I WENT INTO THE HOUSE. THE smell of a Swisher on me made me miss the stink of parmesan cheese that went with it. The reason why I started smoking Swishers to begin with was to get closer to the man who smoked them, whose car reeked of the smell. That front seat, that car, driving around, Cliff loved that car, he loved me too.

Went up into Dad's office. Grabbed Cliff's contact card and went downstairs, grabbed the cordless phone. Went down to the basement, passed the door to the pool, I didn't need escape, I needed Cliff.

Outside, to my area, I lit up another Swisher. Cliff's home phone number was written in the slant of Dad's handwriting.

Clifford Saltzman, home and pager.

Cliff and that pager of his. He'd drive around for hours waiting for that thing to go off.

I didn't know it then, how quickly he'd call back. Barely had enough time to grab a beer from Dad's boat. Just one more. Just this once.

Cliff, he'd been waiting for my call. The phone in my hand rang.

Cliff's breath over the phone, he was with a Client, there was the kind of music Cliff told me people liked to listen to when they wanted to get to know each other better. The kind of music I'd heard on the other side of people's doors late at night, music to make babies to. I could smell the parmesan from over the phone.

I could see Cliff there pulled up on some curb in front of a payphone somewhere on Collins Avenue with two clients in the back getting to know each other. A motel parking lot, right by the lit-up neon sign with two coconuts.

Cliff's voice when he called me back, a little bit of relief at the end of a long night.

"So you've come back to me," he said. Held out the 'me' extra-long, to make me feel sorry for him, for what I'd done.

"Cliff," I said, the things I'd said, the things I'd done. So far gone I even thought Cliff was against me.

The thing that lived in me, my Little Friend, a piece of him broke out of my chest and floated up to my brain. I was coming back to sorry, I didn't know I had it in me.

"Sorry I was such an asshole," I said.

WITH CLIFF THERE WAS ALWAYS a pause before a lecture. The part of his brain telling me, hey Kid, pull up a chair let me sit you down and tell you about life.

"We all fall down, kid, what matters is how you get back up." Cliff said this to me, like somehow he'd been there before.

"Tell you what," he said, "you buy me one of those Italian delights, and we'll call it even.

THESE LOVEBIRDS GOT ABOUT THIRTY minutes left, I'll see you in forty." There was one last musical note that slid over the phone line before Cliff hung up, a deep down and dirty funk.

There was a place I stood, right in front of the driveway, on Bella Vista. The mangroves so close back there, with new kids falling in with the likes of the Beat-Your-Ass Bryans and the Calebs of the world. And with Cliff coming, I was going back to the best of who I was.

Cliff, when Bonnie rounded the corner at the top end of Bella Vista. One turn down onto the tree-lined street, revving the engine like he always did before turning into our driveway.

The slow way he rolled the window down when he pulled up.

"Good night, sweet prince," he said, like I was still that boy on the first day we met. No one could make me laugh like Cliff could.

Twenty minutes later, we had two meatball subs on the red tray and wax paper of Miami Subs. The hum of the white fluorescents, and the flicker of ceiling fans. Cliff lit up a Swisher before he even sat down.

"This one," he said, "is for digestion."

"The second one," he said, which I haven't ordered yet, is so I don't get hungry late in my shift. All I need is a few red lights on Collins Ave and I can down this baby in seconds flat."

THERE WE WERE, THE TWO of us, Cliff smoking in between bites, blew the smoke above my head and into the ceiling fan. Cliff kept me up to date on the goings on of all his clients.

And then, Cliff did that thing he did. I don't know if it was my face or what, but he started talking about Dad again.

Me, I was conflicted, the version of Dad that Cliff remembered, the Dirty Hippie, that wasn't who Dad was anymore. It was remembering a guy who'd basically abandoned me time and time again back to a gentler time, when he was too stoned to walk home in high school. Who drove that lime green Karmann Ghia out to Fire Island.

One thing I did like though, was how Cliff got sentimental when he talked about Dad like that. This was the closest we ever got to being family.

The jokes, the look on his face, it was just him and me telling stories and eating a goddamned meatball sub, but after what I'd been through, just to have him back, to get back to who we were when we first met, that was all I wanted.

Well, that and forgiveness.

WE SAT LIKE THAT FOR a long time. Cliff leaned forward with a Swisher in his hand, big cloud of smoke going up over him. Cliff not saying a word, looking at me like I wasn't there, like he was already thinking about the next client.

Forgiveness. For the things I said and did to him. He wasn't going to just turn and forgive me just like that.

But he did, broke that silent stare with a laugh so big and loud, he almost coughed up a lung while he was doing it. Cliff always did have a shitty poker face.

"I'm glad you came to your senses kid." Cliff said. I didn't know if it was the smoke or what, but it kind of looked like he was about to cry.

Cliff, just being back with him, with someone who was willing to sit and smoke and really listen to what had happened to me.

"I am too," I said, and for a second, I felt like my old self again.

That night, after not seeing him in a long time, the two of us, we were back, like the old times, but better.

POSTCARDS

POSTCARDS, THAT'S HOW I got through the next stretch. The day after I'd buried the hatchet with Cliff, I went out to check the mail. Out on the driveway, I stuck my hand in the mailbox built into the coral wall. There was something wide and tall and sturdy in there, a postcard.

A postcard, which was usually an ad for water heaters or a two-for-one coupon, but when I pulled this one out, it was a plain white postcard.

It took me a few seconds, but when I did figure out what it was and who it was from, it was like, for a second, Mom was standing in front of me in her black dress, home from dinner and drinks, the smoke of her skin and the smell of the whiskey she drank.

The line looped up from left to right in a bulbous shape, an abdomen of a bug with extra shading, her line looped over to the other side and came to a fish hook point, then settled into a long skid of a landing.

On the back was a place to write my name and address, and a dark inkblot for the stamp from some conceptual artist. The slant in the spelling of my name, in the letters, her handwriting, just seeing that, she sat down and drew something for me. That *I* she drew, that was the way she saw me: a little fancy, well-constructed, but with plenty of shading. It took a special kind of love for mom to write me a postcard. Granted it was just one letter, but correspondence with Mom was always going to be cryptic.

The postmark on the card got smudged by the rain or by the sweat of the mailman when he dropped it in the box, so I couldn't see where it was sent from, but really what did it matter. Mom sent *me* a card, and not just one card, but a series of cards.

After the first one with the I on it, they started coming every month. And Mom being Mom, the cards weren't the kind of how-are-you-doing-and-are-you-eating-any-real-food type of card that most Moms send to their sons.

Mom sent me straight lines, long loopy lines, lines with or without a crack in it, an egg with two bird's legs sticking out of the bottom. Regardless of what they had on them, though, the centered around one single letter of the alphabet.

On afternoons after school in the hours before Dad was home with Nora I went down to my room at the bottom of the pool. Down there with my bare feet on the rocks, the curve of the edge of the pool, the path around the slab, looking through the little window where if I walked up close enough I could see up to the patio.

Or if I sat down on the rocks I could look up at the bended edges of light and water, I thought about where among all the postmarks Mom might be coming from, the red branches of the mangroves I couldn't quite see across the street turned into the adobe red of Santa Fe, New Mexico, or a ferny crag on the California coast. In my head I saw Mom painting in a floppy hat, an empty room with a view, one suitcase and an easel to paint her long looping postcards.

For month two's postcard I was expecting the start of a new word, or maybe even a whole word, but instead all I got was an apostrophe, just a mark, with cut outs of Florida oranges, the whole page really a close up of an orange rind glistening in the sun, dark pores of orange skin, and a big black apostrophe mark cut out from a different magazine.

When I got sick of hiding in my sanctuary, I started wandering the neighborhood, looking for abandoned construction sites.

THE NEXT WEEK I GOT the "M," this time the "M" started out as a charcoal line, but the vines entwined themselves all around the cutouts of other "Ms" that made up the rest of the postcard. The M stood on a series of cut outs of alligators, with an ocean behind it.

Over the next few weeks Mom sent the rest of the phrase to me, the rest of the postcards were a series of cutouts with a single letter on it, each featuring a different South Florida motif. There was a flamingo one, a Jai Alai one, and the Calle Ocho themed Cuban one, strands of smoke from different Cuban cigars made up the final E.

As for what I'M HOME meant, maybe she was trying to tell me she was close by, even if she wasn't. Maybe she was getting closer to me psychically, and her art was how she was speaking to me, was how she always spoke to me. Maybe she was in my head and could read my thoughts. Maybe the window at the bottom of the pool was a window to Mom, too. And then again maybe it was just that the idea of Mom with all these postcards was now closer than she was since that last night in Park Slope. Either way she was back in my life, hovering around me, letting me know she hadn't forgotten. When I got the last one, I spread out the whole series on my floor with the door locked, the whole I'M HOME stretched across my floor.

This hope, always Mom and the hope and most of the time it was false, an opening in my chest, that she'd come back soon. Like one night Cliff would drop me off, and there would be Mom standing in our driveway. Her standing there with open arms, saying, come here, kid, let's start the whole me and you thing all over again.

As for how close she was, it was hard to get a read on that, because the mail was never postmarked from Brooklyn, but from as far as Oregon and Washington, and other times, New Mexico, Arizona, or Texas. I never knew if she actually sent these cards from these locations. But I knew she was thinking of me.

I kept these postcards safe, never showing them to Dad, I kept them in a drawer, tied up. I took them out each night when I slept in the empty house, they made me feel less lonely and that one day soon I would see her again.

AND THEN THERE'S AN OPENING

AND THEN ONE DAY, I found it, this opening to my new world. There was only room for me in my world, maybe Cliff on a good day, and then I discovered there was room for somebody else.

I was still wandering the construction sites towards the front part of our subdivision, walking up one of my favorite half-finished staircases, my portable cassette player grinding through all of my mixtapes taped off of college radio. All told there were no less than one thousand sad songs.

I was smoking a Swisher, of course, the late Saturday afternoon sun coming in through the gauzy sky. The chill of early Fall in the air. I heard her moving through one of the window panes upstairs in a soon to be Spanish villa type McMansion, the sound of lumber boards banging away, looked up through that unfinished window pane and there she was, crouched down in front of the scattered woodpile, the shaft of a white cigarette hanging out of her mouth. I waved to her, my arm feeling a little self-conscious up in the air like that, she looked at me for a second, then frowned and returned to her work.

And in this new world of mine we were the only two people trying to figure out civilization by digging through its foundations. She had on overalls with ghostly white base makeup. She had a frown that had always been a part of her face. You could tell how her chin was used to that closeness to her lips that it had been there since birth.

I went down to where she was and before I even got there she was offering theories on the world at large.

"They say you can find out a lot about the society we live in by what they throw away," she said. "All of this stuff here is just scrap to them."

She looked up at me, but really she was really looking up at the sky, addressing whoever might be listening, even though the only person standing here was me.

She spoke to me in a low voice, far away from the rules of conversation, of personal space, her forehead was sharpened to a point with that hair of hers pulled back. "You could build a home in Mexico to fit four people with the amount of shit they are throwing away."

Her name was Michelle, and she was an artist.

"Probably the only one in the neighborhood," she said. "If not in the whole South Miami clusterfuck."

Michelle was searching for materials for her first art installation, and because she worked in multimedia, she was using wood planks that she would eventually paint, bits of old drywall crumbled over a canvas and painted over.

For all of her postmodern aesthetic choices, the way she dressed made you think otherwise. She had white overalls, a flower-patterned blouse underneath every stitch of cloth on her was squarely tucked into the other.

Her mom was an artist too.

"Mom died six months ago," Michelle said, and her frown-shaped mouth went a little bit more towards her chin. "And I am making a fitting tribute to her life and legacy" she told me.

And even though I was liking her more and more the more I talked to her, and how different she was from the rest of the neighborhood. She didn't find me as fascinating as I found her. And even though she talked to me, I could tell, in the way her hands were in her pockets, not letting me see those mawed cuticles on the end of her fingers, the way she backed up at least two paces whenever I walked up to talk to her, that she kept a safe distance.

Each time we met up, it was a chance encounter, she got what she needed, whether it was the planks of wood, or the little pieces of drywall and brick. She loaded them onto her bike, and she was off.

When I told her that I was interested in seeing some of her stuff, she said

"I am really in the middle of my grand inspiration, I don't have time for dates," she said it knowing what it took for someone like me to ask her, she felt a little sorry for me, but she was too gone into her mourning to let herself get involved.

She was old-fashioned and funny in her own way, and maybe it was the sadness in me relating to all that was missing in her. But there was something about her demeanor, the way she had to grow up just to fill in the spaces her mom left behind.

Maybe because of what she went through, she was the only person in my life who didn't lie to me. From the way her white Keds were tied so tight to the way her short shoulder length hair was pulled back by a plastic white hair band that she wore like a halo around her forehead, every part of her was in mourning

And the way she lifted up those boards, looked through each pile, like if she had enough time, with just her and the confines of the various trash piles, she could find all the things she lost when she lost her mother. She could find all the things that she needed in the trash heaps of Bella Vista.

But this opening, the way I was going through the motion, not knowing that someone like that existed in this world, just knowing that someone out there like Michelle was out there was to me, a revelation.

Michelle wasn't out to kick ass, or rob people. Michelle wanted out of this whole society as much as I did.

So that's where I saw her in my world, a club with a membership of two, me and her against the hypocrites and liars that made up the rest of the world. The quiet in those construction sites, this calm place, where in the destruction of all the rich and the beautiful we could find ourselves.

Bella Vista

PARAMOURS

MICHELLE TOOK TO SMOKING like a champ. She might have been seen with a Marlboro dangling from her lips before, but it was just for show. So after running into each other a few times at the construction site, It took her coming over to my place to actually give smoking a try. I was somehow able to convince her that she had to see that bottom of my pool, how much she would love the color. And it did, the way her face, the way those down turned lips of hers turned to an almost smile, the colors coming through that window, a shade of blue found only in the farthest reaches of the pacific ocean, a fantasy color so pure the way it came out of that little window we could look through. I'd said earlier that it was the closest thing I had to church, but what she got out of it, was something I'll never forget.

Her whole body changed when she looked into that little window. It may not have lasted for a long time, but her face reflected back to me through the window, her eyes lit up. This must be the way she looked at a canvas, reserving her attention for those deserving of it, not just throwing it away like most people.

Then we made our way downstairs through the ping pong table room, and the room full of mirrors before Dads workshop room to the back sliding glass doors and on the dock.

The rest of that afternoon was the two of us on that dock smoking, our legs dangling down past the barnacles. After I showed her that window, I got a free pass, the walls came down, she didn't shut herself off, her spine and everything connected to it seemed looser. In a steady stream of cigarette smoke she had found someone she could share her rebellion.

And then, it happened, at the end of a smoke-filled day and two beers each, she leaned in, she looked up at me and licked her lip for a second, gave it little nibble like she wasn't sure she wanted to do what she ended up doing next.

She leaned in, her eyes up at me then away then back on me, than back the other way, then she did it, she leaned in, and kissed me and I when I say kiss I mean it was the movie star kind, we kissed, with tongues.

How so much can open up when you tongue kiss someone the first time, this thing you have in you and the thing Michelle had, the two of us there, in the middle of that awful South Florida humidity, we found each other out of the ruins of our lives.

How good that felt. The two of us out there smoking, with two beers pilfered from Dad's boat. The way the joy of just knowing her rode on the surface of my spine and seemed to stay there for several weeks afterwards. We rode our bikes to her house. When she said goodbye that day, our day, the day we declared war against everyone else in our grade, in our subdivision. Riding home for me was all about promise, a for real deal feeling of happy flowing through me, that tongue of hers was magic, reached into all my dark places and threw up the floodlights, I was happier than I ever was and maybe ever would be.

And even though she was clear with me the whole time, even though I know she was dealing with the death of someone so influential, how for all of my Mom's absent love, I at least had that moment up in the studio where she really saw me, even if nothing else happened since, we still had that moment.

That floodlight feeling didn't go away. It was there the next day. I couldn't help but think about her all the time, and there weren't any clients whatsoever, and I didn't even ask. Cliff paid sole attention to me, which was everything I wanted, but all I thought about was Michelle.

"The puss on you." Cliff said, "Is got to be because of some skirt."

Bella Vista

ME AND MICHELLE

ME AND MICHELLE, THE two of us and the routine, our routine, our ritual, school or no school. She and I were hand in hand, always hand in hand. She and I and me and her. Never thought it would ever be like this, even the little dark friend inside of me went away whenever we hung out, and we always hung out. She and I up and down Bella Vista, making out in the mangroves, the same spots me and Caleb and Beat-Your-Ass Bryan hung out. They were gone though, don't know what happened to them.

This thing rising up between us, this two people make a third thing, she didn't hold anything back. For the first few weeks she didn't talk much and I didn't mind, I was happy that she and I could just share space, and time. On the dock, looking out at the boats in the back of houses, how at the end of the one street, you could see downtown Miami. On those rocks, with Swishers and pilfered beers, she told me about her Mom, about how much she missed her. About how it got her thinking about death, about how much she wanted to be here.

"I didn't want to be alive," she said, "until I met you."

The curve of her lip, the possibility of a smile wrapped in a frown but she did smile, a bit, before the frown took back her mouth, and then I went in.

The kiss, when we kissed, two people together made a third thing. Those feelings, a light burst of air through my brain and down to my chest, heavy down in my pants, this feeling like I was flying yet on the ground more firm than I'd ever been before. This physical feeling of tongues together, but in my head it was what some people could call religion, this love of an idea and the idea is a person and the person is the person in front of you, and she is Love and Love is kissing you, it's the only thing I wanted to do. A kiss when I woke up and rode my rusted out shitty BMX over to her house, a kiss in the mangroves, a kiss in the hallway at school, when we went to school. Easier to see the school day as opportunities to walk and to talk and to kiss and to kiss and to kiss. Days and days of this and what it was doing to the little dark thing that had lived with me since the first time I saw that godforsaken bird lying on its back all those years ago was starting to go away altogether. When I was kissing her, or talking, telling her everything, holding nothing back, words and phrases tumbled out of my mouth, like cash and we broke in and, maybe this guy is a drug dealer but I'm not sure, but it got me down here and it brought me to you.

The two of us on those rocks and her telling me that it was me that kept her alive after her Mom died.

"I'd thought about killing myself so many times, I even tried it once." What she said and how it matched up with what I did.

"The doctors say I'm depressed but what the fuck do they know."

Depressed, that was it, it was a thing in her and it was a thing in me too.

My life was so empty and without much of anything, just a pursuit of booze and smoke one day after the other and feeling like I'd been punished for choosing my father over my mother, then I met Michelle and someone just turned the lights on. I had words, actual words that a doctor could use to tell what was wrong with me, this wasn't some supernatural black cloud that had taken over me, I wasn't covered in death.

I was a depressed teenager, I was a walking fucking cliché, but not when we were together, for the first time I saw how this kind of love was different than the kind of love I got from Cliff, this kind of love went way beyond the "I want to take care of you" kind.

This was the kind that was all encompassing. I wanted to spend every breath with her, from the first moment of the day until the last breath before I started snoring.

I didn't see Cliff for those two weeks, I didn't see anyone, didn't want to see anyone else, just her, just me and Michelle.

I wanted to be like that, forever.

I didn't know then, on those rocks on that day that she told me how I'd saved her, I didn't know that could all just go away because someone changed her mind.

She didn't see me as a lover, she saw me as an enemy. A distraction that would prevent her from living her life. The exact fucking opposite of needing each other.

A phone call, it all ended with a phone call.

"It's not that I don't love you, I do, you've done so much," she said. "But I miss my Mom and I'm kidding myself with you."

The image I was forming in my mind, of her and I holding hands, both of us dressed for some formal thing in the kind of photo I could put on my desk when I got my shit together. That picture fell off the goddamned table.

"I don't need you, I can't be with you, it's taking me away from the work I need to do. I'm not at school when I'm with you, I'm not in my life. I need you too much." she said, her voice turning and breaking, a voice that slid into tears, into the hole I couldn't climb out of. "And that's what scares me, and that's why we can't be together."

"I don't want to see you, not even as friends, Jay, you're just too good, but you've got something inside of you that scares me and if we keep seeing each other, we'll destroy each other, you and I, we, are poison."

One phone call. A series of numbers punched onto a phone's keypad, maybe they have lights under them, these buttons, maybe they are old and raised with white lettering, the phone's handle to your ear, one long copper wire that connects one person to another, not digital, not yet, this was real deal analog, how else could I see this as anything more than a death. How could I get up and face the next day after knowing what life could feel like. How could I pick myself up if I didn't even want to be alive anymore?

She was right, me, I was poison, always was, and back then I thought I always would be.

Bella Vista

MICHELLE MADE ME

A VIEW I NEVER SAW. Me lying on the concrete, looking up after I jumped. At the flap of the screen I cut with the largest knife in the house, the square metal plates at the bottom of my curtains clattering into each other.

Waking up was coming back.

I thought I'd died. But I didn't die. I jumped, from a window, on purpose. I fell face first.

Broke my face, bones and teeth, my cheekbones had to be rebuilt with rods and pins and insurance money. But now that I'd done it, I had to wake up and deal with the part of me that wanted me dead.

What made me almost die for close to an hour was Michelle.

That whole kissing me for two weeks thing, it wasn't real.

She and I were no good for each other, we were poison, that's what she said.

That feeling coming home after I first met her, that I meant something to someone. That someone chose me. That feeling was all that I had in me.

I didn't have anything left, so I had to leave.

I was a slave to that other part of me that wanted me gone, this part of me didn't just appear, the dark in me that had been there since the morning I saw Deadbird Redbird. This was always going to happen.

I had to die.

After I jumped, after I'd laid there for an hour before a neighbor called an ambulance. After I was admitted to the hospital and put in a room. In my head I was still awake and looking up at my room and the mess I'd left behind.

Me on the seawall with two white boat carriers on either side of me. Looking up at my room, at the ceiling fan still going, my blinds blowing out like strands of hair out to the gray sky.

Jumping like I did, from my window down to the seawall, the side of me that wanted to end it all. That part of me, he won that night.

The night we kissed, after she left, I felt more alive than I ever had. I was home in the dark, with no one around to care if I was past curfew, no Cliff, no Mom, no Dad, no nobody, because nobody loved me, because it was me, it was mine, it was my fault.

Really, all of it was my fault.

I knew Mom on drugs wasn't my fault and Dad leaving me behind to a guy he barely knew wasn't my fault. And Michelle not loving me, she was sixteen, who the hell is up for lifelong love at sixteen?

But that night I went up to my room and the stars on my ceiling were a sick green glow and when I woke up the next morning I knew it was time to go.

Wasn't that just everything? Wasn't Michelle telling me on that day, in her dress, in the house that was half finished. The construction site of the house that wasn't built was the connection between her and me. Didn't I know exactly what I was going to do when I woke up that morning and saw those two white cranes against the dark of the seawall, couldn't I have seen the ambulance and me being loaded onto it.

Those two white cranes had pulleys on them that would lift boats up and out of the water. Those two things were things that could carry me to the next world, to a place where I wouldn't hurt anymore.

I saw the plan in front of me, of what I had to do. A dream I already knew the ending to. The handle started with my hand on the handle, pushed down on the switch, slid the window open and let the humid air in.

Pulled far enough for me to fit through. Then the screen, the rows of black webbing that kept the bugs out. I went downstairs to the kitchen and got the biggest steak knife in the house to cut this screen open with.

Downstairs, the door to Dad's wing of the house was closed like it always was. Dad wasn't here, away with Nora, newlyweds and "I'll be a better man from now on."

Down the marble hallway, cold on my feet, through the swishy door to the kitchen, that knife sat there in the drawer, in a knife block. The shadows of blades and silver circles on the handles, pulled that out, the reflection of me in the knife was too dull for me to see.

That knife, the screen, I took that knife and cut a square into it, a doorway within a window, a big square flap for me to walk through.

The part of me that wanted me gone, the thing that started in my chest was all over me, I could feel it going through my veins, lungs, spine, down to toes and feet, up to my spleen, then wiggled its way between my beast bone and through my lungs with each breath I took.

It was all right there, there was no turning back. I'd seen it all in my head already, all I had to do was step though.

When I did jump, it wasn't so much a jump as it was a walk off. When my feet were on the tiles of the roof, that little overhang before it stepped off down to the seawall.

I stepped off the overhang face first.

I could see it all. Didn't close my eyes.

Michelle, that day on the rocks you held my hand and you kissed me. There was this wave that came over me on that day. You breathed life into me. This was something different from the pool pump breathing, different than Mom painting me. With you there was this combo feeling of love and lust rising up in me.

You chose me, Michelle, the day we ran into each other at the construction site of the half-finished house we hung out at. It was cold, cold for Florida, the one week a year you needed to wear a sweater. You didn't have a sweater, so I gave you mine, and you put it on, and there was a little bit of the pink flower pattern on navy blue poking out of the head hole of your sweater.

And you put your hand around my shoulder, pulled me in, you touched my cheek and pulled my face closer to yours. You looked me in the eye and saw the look on my face that said if you did kiss me, it would mean forever.

You knew all of this and you did it anyway, took your lips to my lips and there was a little bit of give and take to our kiss, it wasn't rushed, it was like chewing on delicious food, but I couldn't bite down with my teeth. I had to chew, with my lips.

And you got this look on your face, it was the only time I had ever seen you smile. And after your Mom was gone and your Dad didn't listen to you, it didn't matter anymore, because right at that moment, with the cold chill in the November air, you were mine.

Bella Vista

IMPACT

I DIDN'T CLOSE MY EYES until right before one hundred and seventy-six pounds of me walloped onto concrete. Force and wind and textbook science greeted me, face first.

I don't remember hitting the ground.

Went down nose first, shattered places I didn't know were shatterable.

I broke my face in eighty-five places, eighty-five screws. I don't know how many rods connected to those eighty-five screws. Bruising on my forehead, my chin shattered, part of the eighty-five.

So much time had passed. I had no idea how long, one day or two weeks. I was amazed I even woke up at all.

After I stepped off my roof and went face first down into the concrete, after I held my eyes open for as long as I could before blacking out.

And it was death in a way, if death is blacking out for so long you can't remember. I wasn't living or dead. I was out there, just a brain floating around. There were a few flashes here and there, but only for a second, flashes of tubes and doctors in face masks, a penlight held to my eyes. Left, right. To see if I responded.

The moment I woke up, when I first came to, my mind scanned my body, *How are you doing, How are you feeling.*

There was a raw nerve of pain around my face that had been tapped into but was covered up by the drugs I was probably on. I didn't even know I had a face. There was so much numb around any part of my brain. I had this feeling like my face wasn't there, that it'd been shaved off, my nose, my chin.

I didn't know where I was and I didn't want to open my eyes. I didn't want to see what I'd done to myself.

Waking up, the first thing I heard after a long while of quiet was a beep. My hand was on a crumpled mound of sheet. The first thing I'd touched since I held onto that screen before I stepped off my roof.

I woke up to the beep from some kind of monitor computer-thing plugged into me.

Waking up wasn't as easy as opening my eyes and rejoining the world. It was slower than that. When I first opened my eyes, it was so bright it hurt my eyes. I couldn't see anything clear. Took me a few minutes for the blur in front of me to turn into sharp. But there was this light and it had a color. It was this cool aqua. So close to the light at the bottom of the pool, I thought I was down there for a second.

But that day, coming back to a faded aquarium blue color light on the hospital walls.

PUMPED-IN COLD AIR SMELLED LIKE band aids and faded cigarette smoke. The beeps from whatever the machines that did what they did that were next to me.

Something else, too, this hand in front of me I still couldn't quite see, it was still blurry, and someone was in the chair next to my bed. The red nail polish, the hand, it couldn't be her hand. The one that held the brushes.

Her hand. How could I forget mom's hand? Mom.

I thought I was dead. At the time I thought Mom would never come back to me, I couldn't imagine a reality where she was sitting there to my left, and no way was she sitting there in front of me looking sober.

I wanted to soak all of her in for as long as I had her. I hadn't seen her for years and there she was. Mom and that red hair of hers now tightly curled, shorter, some color to her cheeks, a white flowing dress, her legs crossed, her sandals. Shiny bright red on her fingernails on the hand that held my hand.

Me holding Mom's hand was the only thing I wanted. To have Mom see me.

How many times did I want her around? In the mangroves with Caleb and Bryan. Those crazy nights with Cliff in a limousine with crazy people at four in the morning. All the things I had to figure out on my own.

All the time spent trying to figure out what those postcards meant. The places she'd been: Pittsburgh, Pennsylvania, Redding, California, Portland, Oregon, then all of a sudden a big gap of them, then close, then Savannah, GA, and Tampa, FL.

And then I jumped.

And now she was here. Just seeing her here that was a good thing for me to wake up to. "When I said you were the boy who breaks," Mom said, "I didn't mean it that way." A look in her eyes, a wink, making fun of her old ways. She wasn't lost to the universe anymore.

Seeing her there answered so many of the questions I had for her.

She was sober. She had a coffee in the hand she wasn't holding on to mine, she still smelled of cigarettes and for once I didn't mind.

"I got your postcards," I said.

Mom leaned over to look out the window. I couldn't see what she was looking at, but I bet she was thinking about what happened in between her leaving and me waking up.

"I'm not proud of how long I was gone for," she said. "I was always going to come back. The postcards were my way of doing it," she said.

"For now let's be happy you're still here, the rest can wait until later."

Mom swung her purse around, she hit me in the arm, but only a little bit. Mom, a crinkle and the red arrow going up her soft pack of cigarettes, all loud and crinkly from the cellophane. She was looking at me, kind of the way she used to.

"It took me a long time to get straight," she said, looking around the place, up and down a dip of chin when she looked up at the ceiling and blew the smoke into the slats of a vent that was right above her.

"I had a pretty good thing going with my art and I blew it," Mom said. "When we left, the good stuff went with us."

"I blew it with you, too," she said.

Bella Vista

WHY WON'T YOU STAY?

THE MORNING OF DAD'S wedding. I'm up early to have a smoke in my room underneath the pool. Bright ocean blue watercolor dancing on the white walls. The gravel, the humidity. I was going to miss this place. My jaw, my face, when I smoke I feel every pin and rod, all eighty-five of them, eighty-five parts of what was once broken.

I was up early for once for Dad's wedding. The last few months things had settled down with him, he was home more than he'd been. And sure, all that happened with him and me, we were always going to be distant. But the last few days since I got out of the hospital, he'd been around. She had too. Nora. She was nice enough. She loved my father, she really did. It was in the way she stood, the way her smile hung on her face. Dad, he was calmer, the little things didn't bother him as much.

And I didn't know about any of Dad's money problems. How this house just cropped up with a pool. Anyone who knows anything about finance and how to run a business knows you don't start in the lap of luxury if you have a chance of being successful, but what did I know? The point was I was up early for Dad.

Walked out of that room, my safe place, my sanctuary. Closed the chunk of wood around that little door down in the basement. Walking by the ping pong table, the room of mirrors I wasn't scared to look into.

I wasn't afraid, every mirror reminded me of my new face, my new life. For the first time in a long time, there was this fresh feeling I had down in my chest, a welcoming newness.

Upstairs on the couch. Put the TV on. Felt the AC on my neck where my necktie was tied a little too tight. The humidity downstairs, the sweat starting to dry a little bit. The usual crap on TV, hundreds of channels, I got lost in keeping track of all the unhappy people on all the unhappy channels.

Then over by my left eye I saw them, the black in Dad's tux. The black in Nora's dress. Like the two of them, they were somehow remembering my Mother. It was like she was dead, which was strange, but at least they were thinking of her.

Nora and Dad through the sliding glass door. The screen door opens up and there they were ready for their next adventure. Nora, she came over to me, put her hand on the back of my neck over to where the too-tight feeling was. Her face there over mine, her smile and the way the rest of her face was built around that smile.

As for my own, it was still a bit of a mess. But people could tell I was well. So I was ok with it.

"They did a great job with your face." Nora drew a quick circle with her finger.

"We're about ready to go."

Dad behind her, his hands over her shoulders. He let her do the talking, so much between us and how do we talk about it. Something else too, a lightness in him, some might even have called it relaxation. I just called it happy. Even with all we'd been through, at the end of the day it was nice to see him happy.

I get up to go, and Dad, he moved in front of her, he's got his hand out for me to shake, like this whole thing is some kind of business deal.

"I'm so glad you could be here," Dad said, and in the back of his eyes, they were a little shiny where the tears had started and stopped.

All the things he said with that handshake, those eyes and their not quite a cry. The whole line of Pershall men that couldn't talk about their feelings. The darkness is him in me and in Daddy, his Dad. I didn't know it then, this was Dad saying how proud he was of me. For turning it around.

And maybe, somewhere in the back of his mind, he was sorry.

WE ALL WENT IN DAD'S car, the rattle of Dad's diesel Mercedes. The clean smell. Classical music on the radio. Today was strings, strings and the slow of Dad pulled out onto Bella Vista.

The wedding was at this old hotel that Al Capone used to stay in. The place had a buffet that stretched across three rooms, no fooling, lobster and shrimp, carving stations with guys who had chef's hats on, the works. Made to order, whatever you want.

The Ceremony, the two of them by the pool, whole stands and rows of seats empty. Who gets married in front of a pool with stands, where people can watch other people swim?

It was a nice ceremony, only a few of Dad's clients and Cliff, naturally. We sat in the stands, and Cliff brought these pistachio nuts. Like he's at a ballgame in Brooklyn, like the old days never went away.

The moment, the kiss, and Dad looking happier than I'd seen him since he was the Dirty Hippie. Dad, and the always smile that was on his face in those days. He'd found his home in Nora, and now it was time to find mine.

After the wedding, after all the champagne toasts and me having some. Cliff with his hand on my shoulder, parmesan and sweat.

"The kid's almost eighteen, let the boy have some."

DAD AND ME AND NORA, at the end, when everybody else had gone away. "Cliff tells me you are headed North tomorrow, Carolina, isn't it?" Nora, she wasn't my Mom, but she did care about me.

"In the morning, yeah, Cliff's taking me."

"**I**F IT WASN'T FOR OUR honeymoon," Dad said, I would've taken you to college." Dad, when he said that, there wasn't all that dark in him then, there was something else in there. One of those coded phrases, somewhere in there in Dad was regret. Hey, he said, he had his hand on my shoulder like he does when he wanted to tell me this is something you'll remember in ten years' time. And Dad, there's something funny with him because he's starting to shake a little. It's there in his chest and it's in the shiny in his eyes, only this time, there are tears coming, and crying, sobbing, eyes turned down at the corners.

"I'm sorry I was such a shitty father," he said.

PORTALS, THEY COME UP SOMETIMES. You are walking around in life and there are moments that open up to other moments, so you can see this hole through to where it started, at the beginning. All those times I was alone when I shouldn't have been. All those scary days in the back of the Limo. All the father figures who raised me. All the things I had to figure out on my own.

And something else too. A clearing in me. The shake in my chest because I knew it was coming too, the wrongs that were so wrong, how much I hated him and didn't even tell myself just how much. Just kept on hating him until I didn't love him anymore, expecting nothing but him not being there.

And now, this.

IF I WAS GOING TO start fresh, I had to let go of this thing, this darkness that jumped out of me, the hating my Dad, it was all I knew how to do anymore. I could feel it down there, the hated, burning up so it was all I felt, I blamed everything bad in who I was on him not being there, for smothering out any feeling of self I might've had.

Turn a corner, if you want to turn a corner, you have to admit that you were wrong. "It's okay Dad. "You did what you had to do. You built all this. It was hard, but I got through it. I forgive you."

And I know, I couldn't have just given up all the hate I had for my father. But when a guy his age, a baby boomer, has the balls or whatever to admit he was a shitty father, you thank him for that thing that so many men don't ever get a chance to do. I let it slide, I told myself that the things I said were true. It was such a nice day, why spoil it. I had the rest of my life to let it go.

I'm still working on letting it go.

I gave him a hug. I know, me mister darkness, and him, my father, Dad, Mr. Doom and Gloom reached my hands around his chest, and the bit of stomach that always stuck out a bit. The smell of his English leather cologne, and somewhere in there, mothballs. And Nora got close to us, stood behind me, and wrapped her arms around me, and around Dad, around us. And for the first time in years, I was in the middle of something you could call family.

FIN

SOME MORNINGS YOU WAKE up and know it's going to be a bad day, something about the way the blood settles in your body. The why and how it moved through your veins.

Other days, there are other days when you know it's going to be the day. The last day.

THE VIEW COULDN'T BE MORE perfect out my window, bright sun, no clouds, the two boat lifters and the seawall, like I never had a thought in my head other than the one I had then.

And today that thought was getting out, was starting over. All my stuff was already packed. Dad and Nora were gone on some honeymoon somewhere. I pulled out my drawer, took Mom's wedding ring. Slid it on my fattest finger, turned it up so the diamond hit the sun coming in from my window.

I'd packed everything the night before into one large duffel bag I called the super sausage.

Carrying it downstairs, the little squeaks on the stairwell were telling me I was getting out. This place, this dream, it isn't Dad's, it's yours.

Downstairs by the pool, through the window. There's Cliff out there. He's got his full on limo drivers suit on. The hat too. He's smoking a Swisher. It's in his mouth, he's biting down on that plastic end. He's got it in his mouth so he can clap with the other two hands. Clapping, just clapping and biting down on that Swisher of his.

The humidity still smacked me in the face when I opened up that door. On the last day. No time for breakfast because it's a ten-hour drive up north. Going north to go South. My college, my new town, Columbia, South Carolina, where people say hello when you walk by.

That last day on the patio. The way that house looked compared to the first time, the patio, the Jacuzzi off, the cover on it. The tennis court we never used. The view wasn't beautiful, until the end. Nothing was as sweet as locking the door, the pull on my shoulders, from the big sausage duffel bag. The two of us on that last day. Cliff and I, walking out.

I put my key in the mailbox. The empty rattle it made when I closed it.

I turned around and there was the Limo. I don't think I'd ever seen Bonnie so washed and ready. I went to sit in the front, but Cliff had other plans.

"Nuh uh, not today," Cliff said, that smile of his hid some kind of a big surprise. "Today, sir, Master Jay, you are riding in the back."

His eyes, they got this shiny thing to them, a heavy gloss to those marbles. "Today you're the client."

The back, the part of the Limo I barely ever got to see, the leather seats with their shine, the glasses by the bar. The sci-fi sound that partition made when it opened up. And this time it opened up for me. Because there was Cliff on the other side, starting ol' Bonnie up.

Because she purred like a Bonnie.

"This is for you kid." Cliff puts on the radio. Marvin Gaye. "Got to give it up."

BUT BEFORE I LEFT, BEFORE we pulled out with me riding client style, I had to see this thing, this house, this Bella Vista.

What it means and what it meant. Beautiful view and how that beautiful view changed with me. How what seemed so big on that first day didn't seem so big anymore. The two-story window, with the carpeted stairs, the patio and all the rooms that came off of it. My chapel under the pool, all the things that made me. It wasn't beautiful until I left it behind. Through the tinted windows I saw it as we pulled out, down the street to the tree-lined street of Bella Vista. Beyond that, the road, the highway, the state, college and the rest of my life. And how through all of it, Cliff was the one person who never stopped caring about me.

Down Bella Vista, we turned right out of the subdivision, then onto the road that led us to the highway that led us out of Miami.

A few hours later, we were up somewhere far north, Jacksonville, then the state line. And Cliff waits until we are out of Florida to say it, of course.

Opened up the partition to talk to me. The nonstop R&B finally stops. The music off, Cliff's hat on his head, he turned to me.

"You're like a son to me, you know that."

Cliff, wasn't just saying it to say it, he had tears in his eyes.

"Today, you're not a boy. Today you are a client. Today you are a man."

And for the first time ever I felt like one.

ACKNOWLEDGMENTS

Enormous thanks to Lisa Kastner at Running Wild Press for making a dream come true.

Thanks much to Peter Wright, my steely-eyed editor for getting me through the last steps.

I'd like to acknowledge my wife Janet for all of the love and support over the years it took to bring this book to life. To my two beautiful daughters Lily and Zoe, who I cradled to my shoulder while working on early drafts.

To James Gill and Noah Hale, my earliest writing champions.

To my current Pinewood Squares members, Pat Janowski, Pat Jewett, Carol Fischbach, Steve Denniston, Marc Cozza, Kristi Lovato, to all Pinewood Table-rs, Dangerous Writers, to Kyle Delamarter, Ray Jicha, Jenn Ellis, Bryce Baxter and David Katz.

To my writing mentors, Tom Spanbauer & Michael Sage Ricci. To my Dangerous Writer Community, to Colin Farstad for being my first reader for Bella Vista, for Brad Rosen and all of his insightful comments, To Matty Byloos for publishing Deadbird Redbird in Nailed Magazine, and teaching me so much about line editing. To Kathleen Lane for the feedback and support, to my forever Burnt Tongue compatriot, Domi Shoemaker, to Gigi Little, Doug Chase, to Stefan Lombard, to Shannon Brazil, Holly Goodman,

Elva Redwood, John Hinds, Krista Price, Acacia Blackwell, Christy George, Margaret Malone, Wes Griffith, and Kevin Meyer.

To those blurbers who blurbed *Bella Vista*: Joanna Rose, Gigi Little, Anne Gudger, Kathleen Lane, Jenny Forrester.

To those who offered words of advice, Laura Stanfill, Liz Prato.

To those who have championed my book when I had my doubts: Jenny Forrester, Daniel Elder.

To the greater Portland Writing Community especially Steve Arndt.

For my Mom and Dad, Sister and Brother in Law. I love you all more than words can say.

To all of the students I've taught in the last 20 years of teaching, I hope you see what's possible.

ABOUT RUNNING WILD PRESS

Running Wild Press publishes stories that cross genres with great stories and writing. RIZE publishes great genre stories written by people of color and by authors who identify with other marginalized groups. Our team consists of:

Lisa Diane Kastner, Founder and Executive Editor
Joelle Mitchell, Licensing and Strategy Lead
Reuben Tihi Hayslett, Acquisition Editor, RIZE
Benjamin White, Acquisition Editor, Running Wild
Peter A. Wright, Acquisition Editor, Running Wild
James Aquilone, Acquisition Editor, Monstrous Books

Resa Alboher, Editor
Angela Andrews, Editor
Rebecca Dimyan, Editor
Aimee Hardy, Editor
Cecilia Kennedy, Editor
Barbara Lockwood, Editor

Bella Vista

Kelly Ottiano, Editor

Evangeline Estropia, Product Manager
Pulp Art Studios, Cover Design
Standout Books, Interior Design
Muzammil F., Interior Design

Learn more about us and our stories at
www.runningwildpublishing.com

Loved this story and want more?
Follow us at
www.runningwildpublishing.com/rize,
www.facebook/runningwildpress,
on Twitter @lisadkastner @RunWildBooks